Praise for Cassandra Dean

Rescuing Lord Roxwaithe is sweet, funny, romantic, witty and emotional. A gem of a Regency romance!
– Anna Campbell, author of the bestselling Dashing Widows series

Two stubborn souls clash and sparks fly as their story unfolds beautifully with drama, sensual awakenings, trials and tribulations, and uncertainties makes [Rescuing Lord Roxwaithe] one outstanding read that you won't want to miss!
–Amazon reviewer

I always love reading books by Cassandra Dean, they're sweet, they're fun, they're witty and more than a little steamy.
– Krissy's Bookshelf

Ms. Dean's ability to craft a scene makes it seem as if I'm really there watching everything transpire.
– Plot Twist Reviews

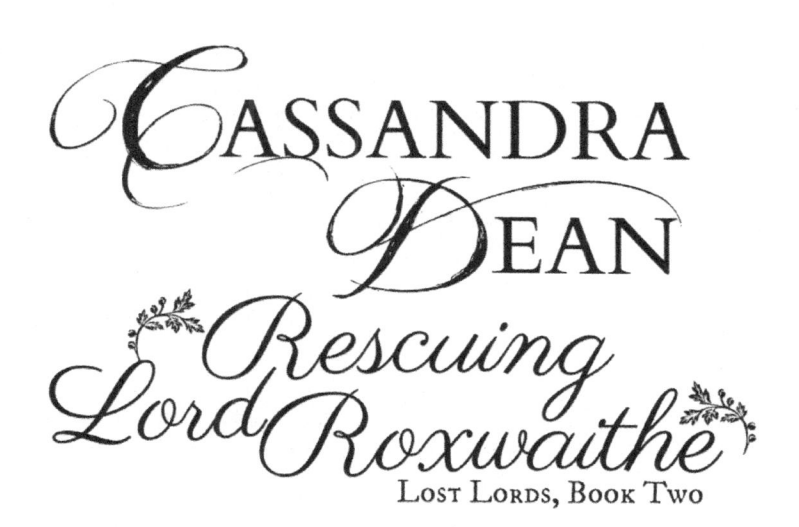

CASSANDRA DEAN

Rescuing Lord Roxwaithe

LOST LORDS, BOOK TWO

Rescuing Lord Roxwaithe
Copyright © 2019 by Cassandra Dean
Print version: Copyright © 2020 by Cassandra Dean

Cover Design: SeaDub Designs
Interior Book Design: SeaDub Designs

Edited by White Rabbit Editing

All rights reserved.
No part of this publication may be reproduced, distributed, or transmitted in any form by any means, including photocopy, recording, or other electronic or mechanical methods, without the prior written permission of the publisher, except in the case of brief quotations embodied in critical reviews and certain other non-commercial uses permitted by copyright law.
This book is a work of fiction. All names, characters, locations, and incidents are products of the author's imagination. Any resemblance to actual persons, living or dead, locales, or events is entirely coincidental.

By Cassandra Dean

Enslaved
Teach Me
Scandalous
Rough Diamond
Fool's Gold
Silk & Scandal
Silk & Scorn
Silk & Scars
Silk & Scholar
Slumber
Awaken
Finding Lord Farlisle
Rescuing Lord Roxwaithe

To OPJ and AAJ
Because I know you'll get a kick out of it.

*Here's to chocolate chip pancakes and banging pots
when Port Adelaide win.*

Love and cuddles

CD

CASSANDRA DEAN

Rescuing Lord Roxwaithe

LOST LORDS, BOOK TWO

Prologue

OLIVER MALCOLM ALOYSIUS FARLISLE, Viscount Hudson and heir to the Earl of Roxwaithe, was fourteen years and one week the day he met Lady Lydia Claire Torrence, youngest daughter of the Marquis of Demartine. It was an unimpressive occasion. She was, after all, only three days old.

"You're squishing her," his youngest brother complained. At six, Maxim barely reached Oliver's chest, but that didn't stop him from tugging at Oliver's arm as if the action would somehow rectify the situation.

"No, I'm not," he retorted, though he gingerly loosened his hold.

"If he were squishing her, she would be crying," Alexandra said. At five, she wasn't much shorter than Maxim, and, as the baby's older sister, she would know better than Maxim if Oliver was squishing Lydia.

Maxim rolled his eyes. "He is too squishing her. Don't defend him, Alexandra."

"I'm not defending him." Brows drawn, she studied her sister. "She is rather red, though."

Oliver loosened his hold even more.

In the corner, the baby's other siblings were currently rolling a ball back and forth. Four-year-old Harry's face was creased in concentration, while at two, George reacted with delight each time he captured the ball.

Oliver shifted the baby in his arms. Alexandra and Maxim crowded closer to him, as if the baby was the most interesting sight they'd ever beheld. He wasn't sure why they thought this. The Marquis and Marchioness of Demartine had produced four children thus far, with Lydia being the youngest. One would suppose they would be used to the arrival of a new baby, but instead Lydia's arrival had been greeted with fascination and—he winced—the stepping on of toes by younger brothers.

In the armchair placed before the nursery window, his middle brother Stephen stared out, his chin on his updrawn knees. At ten, Stephen kept mostly to himself, even when they were all ensconced in the nursery in Bentley Close.

Oliver looked down at Lydia. There would be no more siblings for him. Their mother had died giving birth to Maxim and their father seemed uninterested in providing them with a stepmother. In fact, their father preferred to leave the parenting of them to a series of governesses and tutors, and the prospect of a stepmother seemed unlikely.

The baby shifted in his arms, her small mouth making a moue. In a month, he was to Eton, the first time he'd left Waithe Hall for any length of time since he himself was born. Lydia would change and grow, and the next time he would see her, she would be fat, drooling and healthy, not this wrinkled red thing that had wholly captured the attention of two families.

The door to the nursery opened. Lady Demartine entered, a harried look on her fine features. "Thank you for holding her, Oliver. I'll take her now."

For some reason, Oliver was loath to return Lydia to her mother. Lady Demartine didn't notice, however, taking the baby and expertly swinging her into her arms, wincing a little as the baby pressed against her chest. "You boys should return to Waithe Hall soon. Surely you are expected for dinner."

"Mama, Maxim should stay for dinner," Alexandra said. "And Oliver and Stephen, too."

"Alexandra, their father is expecting them."

"Father is not there," Maxim said, his eyes on Lydia, who was gripping his index finger.

"Where is he?"

Maxim shrugged.

Lady Demartine turned blue eyes to Oliver. "Oliver?"

"I believe he set out for London," he said.

Her brows rose. "Again?"

He resisted the urge to follow Maxim's example and shrug. Their father was often called to London and seemed to have no compunction leaving his children in the care of his old friends. It was the way of things. Their father went to London and they were left in the care of Lord and Lady Demartine. To speak the truth of it, Oliver preferred staying at Bentley Close. The Torrences were raucous and fun, and sometimes Lady Demartine hugged him.

Now, Lady Demartine sighed and rang for the butler. "Simmons," she said once the servant had arrived. "Liaise with the butler and housekeeper at Waithe Hall and organise for Viscount Hudson, Lord Stephen and Lord Maxim to stay with us."

"Very good, my lady. And how long will they be staying?"

"Let us say two weeks, Simmons. They may need to partially shutter the hall. If the servants require direction, we will help with arrangements."

"Very good, my lady."

Once the butler had left, Lady Demartine shook her head before turning to Oliver. "You boys will be comfortable here?"

"Yes, my lady." Of course they would be comfortable. Sometimes, he pretended Lord and Lady Demartine were his parents. Sometimes, he pretended he and Stephen and Maxim could stay at Bentley Close always, but he knew it was only pretend. He knew he would one day be the Earl of Roxwaithe, and he had a duty to his ancestors, to his tenants, and to those who would come after him. He could, fleetingly, pretend, but it was always fleeting and he would never, not in a million years, voice his fancies.

In Lady Demartine's arms, Lydia opened her eyes, and he was caught by her unblinking stare. An unwilling smile tugged at him and, though he knew she was too young, he could swear she smiled in return.

***

OLIVER WAS EIGHTEEN YEARS and two months the summer he finished at Eton. In the autumn, he would begin at Cambridge, but for two months he would return home to Waithe Hall.

The carriage rumbled along. Bracing his foot on the seat opposite, Oliver stared out the window. They'd left Waithe Village ten minutes ago and it would not be long before he would see the turrets of Waithe Hall and, even further in the distance, the chimneys of Bentley Close.

The carriage turned on the drive leading to Waithe Hall and Oliver grinned broadly. Seated on the stump that marked the beginning of the drive was Lydia Torrence. Every time he came home after a length of time, no matter where he'd been, he always found her sitting on that stump, waiting for him. She was only four years old, and yet she somehow managed to escape her governess and her nurse with alarming regularity.

"Myers, slow down," he called. The coachman obliged, coming to a stop before Lydia. "What are you doing out here?" he asked her.

She jumped off the stump. "Waiting."

Fighting his grin, he asked gravely, "For what?"

Big hazel eyes met his. "For you."

It was a ritual between them. He always asked and she always answered the same. He opened the carriage door for her and she clambered inside, seating opposite him. Her feet dangled over the edge.

"Are you back?" she asked.

"For the summer," he said, knocking the roof. The carriage lurched, and then they continued on.

Lydia's small brows drew together. "I don't like it when you go away."

"I don't like going away." He glanced out the window. "I miss this."

"Do you miss me?"

"Of course."

"When I'm older, we'll get married, and then you won't go away."

Laughing, he shook his head. She smiled in return, swinging her feet as the carriage rumbled toward Waithe Hall.

***

OLIVER WAS TWENTY-THREE years and seven months when Maxim died.

The rain had cleared that morning, before the service, but the sky was still murky and grey. Dry-eyed, he stared as they lowered the coffin into the earth. The empty coffin, because Maxim had been lost at sea halfway across the world.

A small hand wormed into his. He glanced down at the top of a strawberry-blonde head. Lydia. The little girl had wormed her way to his side and, though he was loath to say it, he was glad of her company.

Opposite, his father stared at the coffin. Oliver watched him stonily. It was because of him his brother had been on that ship, because of an argument their father refused to discuss. Because of him, his brother was dead.

Beside him stood Stephen, his face wet with tears. Oliver didn't think his brother even realised he cried. Every so often, their father would throw an impatient look at him, scowling at his middle son's emotion, because God forbid someone displayed even a modicum of normal human expression—

Oliver's chest tightened. Stephen wasn't the middle son anymore.

The hand in his squeezed. He felt his lip tremble, felt wetness well in his eyes. Screwing his eyes shut, he willed emotion away. Lydia's hand was warm, comforting, and he focused on the feel of it, the small shape, the sturdy fingers. He could feel the ragged edges of her nails, because she bit them when she was nervous or upset.

God. Upset. Of course she was *upset*. They were all fucking *upset*.

Slowly, people filed past him, murmuring condolences, offering platitudes, and the entire time, Lydia's hand remained in his.

***

OLIVER WAS TWENTY-FIVE years and five weeks when he became Earl of Roxwaithe.

Legs sprawled before him, he watched as his father's valet—no, Bartlett was *his* valet now—fussed around him, preparing a bowl of hot water, shaving soap and towels. The earl's chambers in Roxegate, the family's London townhouse, were his now, as was Waithe Hall, and every one of the properties that comprised the Roxwaithe estate.

Oliver gripped the arm of the chair, the chair that until very recently had been his father's. He supposed he felt some grief his father had died. That must be what this emptiness was, though it felt different from when Maxim had died. This grief was more like indifference, and…relief.

Bartlett mixed the shaving cream, the motions quick and practiced. Oliver rubbed his jaw. Twice a day his father had him shave, and his hair trimmed every Sunday. His clothes were his father's choice, and now his rooms were his father's. Everything in his life was his father's. Nothing was his.

"I will not need a shave this morning, Bartlett," he said abruptly

The valet looked as surprised as Oliver that he'd spoken. "My lord?"

"Help me dress, Bartlett," he continued, trying to sound authoritative. It must have worked, because the valet leapt to action.

Having skipped his morning shave, Oliver's face felt strange as he made his way to the study. His father had often scoffed at those gentlemen at his club who grew moustaches or sideburns, or whose hair was longer than the earl had deemed appropriate.

Sitting behind the earl's desk, he stared at the stacks of paper flanking the blotter that seemed to have multiplied overnight. Roxwaithe owned property in thirteen shires, along with the London town house and the ancestral estates in Northumberland, while the shipping concern sprawled across the globe, with an office in too many ports to count. Keeping the business of Roxwaithe was a job he'd spent his life preparing for but now it had arrived, he knew how woefully inadequate that preparation had been. Some days, it seemed it would never end and he stayed at his desk until the early hours, his eyes gritty as the candles burned low.

His gaze snagged on a particular report. Waithe Hall, the seat of the earldom, was haemorrhaging funds, keeping a full number of staff in preparation for the arrival of an earl who never did. Old pain lanced him at the thought of returning to Northumberland, where every corner held a memory of his youngest brother.

He rang for his secretary and within moments, Rajitha appeared. Rajitha was not his father's man, but instead the one choice Oliver had made. Around

Oliver's own age, Rajitha's dark eyes missed nothing, and he possessed a calm competency Oliver desperately needed.

"Rajitha, instruct the staff at Waithe Hall to shutter the property and close the house," he said.

Rajitha did not react. "Of course, my lord. Do you require anything else?"

"No. Thank you."

After Rajitha left, Oliver exhaled. He rolled his shoulders, feeling as if a weight had been lifted. If he had need to go to Northumberland, he would stay at Bentley Close. Lord Demartine would not object, and thus there was no reason to keep Waithe Hall open. It made economic sense, and the staff stationed there could be better utilised elsewhere. Besides, he was now the earl and he could do whatever he damned well pleased.

The door to his study burst open. Startled, he watched as Lydia exploded into the room. At eleven years old, she'd shot up in the last few months, such that she almost reached his shoulder if they stood side by side.

"What are you doing here?" he asked. He didn't ask how she'd got here. Their townhouses bordered each other, and they'd all long ago discovered the common attic.

"I never see you anymore, so I am here to keep you company." She dragged an armchair opposite his desk and plonked herself in it.

He watched her do so without comment. "Aren't you going to be bored?" he finally asked.

She held up a book, one he knew to be on architecture because he knew Lydia to be obsessed with architecture. "No." Settling in to her chair, she opened the book. "Go on with your work."

He looked at the paper before him and did as she bid. Every now and then, he'd look up to find her completely absorbed in her book, a lock of hair wound around her finger.

Smiling, he shook his head and returned to his work.

***

OLIVER WAS TWENTY-NINE years and ten months when Tom Harding beat Anthony Mulgrave by a straight knock out in the grudge match of the century.

The fight had been the biggest ticket for months. He'd told Lydia yesterday he wouldn't be working in his study today, and she'd been distinctly amused by his ill-concealed excitement. Wainwright had been the one to source the tickets, and Oliver had met his friend at the public house staging the fight. They'd proceeded to match each other ale for ale as they'd joined the throng cheering on Harding and Mulgrave.

The door to Roxegate loomed before him. He missed it the first time he'd tried to rap on it. Damn thing wouldn't stay still. He tried again. His knuckles made contact, but the leather of his gloves made little noise. Squinting, he remembered there was a doorbell. Somewhere. That would probably work better. Bracing himself against the door, he waited until there was only one knocker. Possibly, he may have had a little too much to drink.

Eventually, he managed to find the doorbell. The thing made the most horrific ring, but the door opened and the dour face of his butler filled his vision. Tugging off his gloves, Oliver stumbled into the townhouse, leaving them where they fell while he tugged at his great coat and then his jacket. He struggled with his waistcoat, though, the buttons stubborn bastards, but he bested them in the end, the waistcoat hanging open as he pulled his shirt from his breeches.

"My lord, may I suggest you finish disrobing in your chamber?"

He turned. Arms full of Oliver's discarded clothes, Hood regarded him without expression.

"Yes. Good. That's a good idea." He put his hand to his head. Damn thing was throbbing.

"Very good, my lord." Hood watched him for a moment. "Do you require assistance?"

"Yes, Hood. Thank you." He allowed the butler to lead him to his bedchamber and, once Hood had left, Oliver rubbed the strangely dry flesh of his lip as he tried to put his finger on what he was feeling. He was…. He was something. His skin felt jumpy, and he wanted…he wanted to tell someone what had happened. It had been the greatest thing he'd ever seen and—

Lydia. He wanted to tell Lydia. Maxim always used to sneak into Alexandra's bedroom, so why couldn't he do the same with Lydia?

His chest tightened at the thought of his dead brother, but he pushed those feelings aside. Looking down at himself, he saw he still wore his breeches and boots, though his shirt was untucked and his waistcoat hung open. Somewhat presentable.

It was a short order to stumble from his room and up the stairs to the attic, and even less to lurch to the Torrence side. He managed to be mostly quiet as he stumbled through their hallways, unerringly making his way to Lydia's room.

She was asleep, of course. He stood just inside the threshold of her chamber, vacillating. Should he wake her? She looked so peaceful, but he wanted to tell her.... The room started to spin. He shook his head. Why was it spinning? He put his hand out to steady himself. Something crashed to the floor, the sound muffled by the carpet. A lamp? What was a lamp doing there?

She stirred. "Oliver?" she asked sleepily.

"Lydia." The vague thought crossed his mind that this was inappropriate, but he'd known her forever and Lord Demartine was like his uncle. "I went to the fight, Lydia." The edge of her bed was right there. He sat and ran his hands though his hair. He hadn't pulled it back, and it hung to his shoulders. The room stopped spinning. "It was amazing."

The corners of her lips lifted. "Did you perhaps celebrate?"

He held up his hand, thumb and index finger held an inch apart. Was it an inch apart? He couldn't really focus. "A little. The fight was amazing, Lydia."

Sitting up, she crossed her legs beneath the bedclothes. "Tell me about it."

And, happy to have the attention of the one person in the world whose attention he always wanted, he did.

***

OLIVER WAS THIRTY YEARS and seven hours when Lydia stormed into his breakfast. "Happy birthday," she growled, and then threw herself into a chair.

He lifted his coffee cup to his lips. He knew from long experience not to ask when she was in one of these moods and that it was always best to let her tell him.

He didn't have to wait long. "I don't see why I should learn the pianoforte," she complained. "It is a stupid instrument, and I am bad at it besides."

"It is what all accomplished young ladies learn," he said. "Don't you want to be accomplished?"

She shot him a dirty look. "It is a waste of time. Why do I need these lessons, when I shall be marrying you once I'm old enough?"

He frowned into his cup. She had been saying the same thing since she was a small girl and though he'd tried numerous times to dissuade her, she stubbornly insisted that eventually they would wed. It was right to dissuade her. One day soon, she would realise boys her age were much more interesting and she would forget all about how she'd once wanted to marry him.

Something ached in his chest. He eyed the sausage with distaste. He was too young to suffer a heart complaint, but perhaps he should cut back on rich foods just in case.

"However," she said, dispersing thoughts of early onset heart conditions. "It is your birthday. What should you like to do?"

"I should like to enjoy my breakfast."

As quickly as that, her mood changed and she smiled, dazzling him with its brightness. "Then that is what we shall do." Grabbing a piece of toast, she munched away, grinning all the while.

Shaking his head, he drank his coffee. The funny thing was, there was no other person he wanted to spend his birthday with.

***

OLIVER WAS THIRTY-ONE years and five months when he looked up from his desk, saw Lydia in the armchair opposite, and realised she had become a woman.

She sat in her chair as she usually did, her legs drawn up under her. Her shoes lay discarded on the floor, and she twirled a lock of red-gold hair around her finger as she read yet another book on architecture, writing every now and then in the leather-bound notebook he'd given her for Christmas. He knew the book to be on architecture, because every book in the pile on the table next to her chair was on the same subject. The long line of her thigh was outlined by the flimsy gown, and the turn of her head emphasised the graceful sweep of her neck. Her lips were pink and her teeth bit into the plumpness of the lower one, her lashes dark fans on her cheeks. Her breasts—

Christ. He wasn't going to think about her breasts.

He stood abruptly. "You have to leave."

Startled, Lydia looked up from her book. "Pardon?"

His gaze locked on her lips, which were pink and full and— "You have to leave. Now."

Her brow creased. "Why?"

"Because this is.... It's inappropriate."

"Inappropriate? How is today different from yesterday?"

"Because it is."

"You are making no sense, Oliver—"

"And that's another thing. You should refer to me as Roxwaithe."

Her brows just about shot off her forehead. "Now I know you've gone insane."

He needed her gone. He needed her gone so he could get his thoughts back in order and not think how soft her skin looked. "Please, Lydia. Please leave."

Slowly, she unfolded herself from the chair. "All right, but only because you are acting strange."

Good. Good. He waited impatiently for her to do so.

She stopped. "Mama wanted to know if you would like to come to dinner tonight?"

"Of course." Anything to get her to leave.

She nodded and then gave him the most glorious smile. Something squeezed near his heart.

Once she left, he rubbed the heels of his hands into his eyes. It was an aberration, these thoughts. He was just surprised, was all. He knew she was growing older, knew she would make her debut after she turned eighteen, but he hadn't *known*. Now he did.

Tomorrow, all would be normal. He would look at her, see a woman, and that would be all.

That had to be all. It had to.

***

OLIVER WAS THIRTY-TWO years and four days when Lydia kissed him.

Torrence House was ablaze in light, the ball celebrating Lydia's eighteenth birthday in full swing. Arms behind his back, Oliver stood against the entrance hall wall. From his vantage, he could see into the ballroom while also noting each person who entered. Usually, he'd stand with Wainwright, but his friend had gotten himself married less than a month ago and was currently enjoying his honeymoon with the new Lady Wainwright.

Most of society had turned out for Lydia's birthday ball, and he knew his brother was somewhere in the throng. He hadn't seen Stephen for weeks now and, judging by the crush of people at Torrence House, he wouldn't be seeing him tonight.

He most likely wouldn't see Lydia either. He hadn't seen much of her in the preceding weeks, which was good. It was right. She was preparing for her debut, for dazzling the young men of their set with her wit and her warmth. He would not be surprised if she ended the season with a multitude of admirers, a plethora of proposals, and some young buck's ring on her finger.

His jaw clenched. And that was good. It was right.

"Dancing, Roxwaithe?" Lord Demartine stood beside him. Lydia's father was an imposing figure, his shock of brown hair only lightly sprinkled with grey.

"No, sir," he replied.

"No, you always were more interested in observation." His smile took the sting out of the words. "However, I implore you, find Lydia. All she can talk of is the fact she can dance with you at this ball."

Heat burned his cheeks. "Is it appropriate, sir?"

"I don't see why not." He levelled hazel eyes upon him. "You're a good lad, Roxwaithe. You know timing is everything."

"Sir?"

"Find her, Roxwaithe. Have pity for my ears." He clapped him on the shoulder and left.

Entering the ballroom took only a few steps and there, in the middle of the dance floor, was Lydia. She laughed as her partner whirled her around, her red-gold curls bouncing. She wore a light-coloured gown cut low, her breasts almost plumped. The young men around him stared at her with lust-filled eyes, not that she noticed but he sure as hell did. He scowled.

She caught sight of him and the smile she wore turned radiant. The dance ended and she said something to her partner before she made her way to him.

"Your father said you wished to dance," he greeted her.

"I did. I do. But I should like to show you something first." Wiping her hands on her dress, she licked her lips. "Come with me?"

Distracted by her tongue, he nodded dumbly and followed as she led him from the ballroom. It wasn't until she'd led him to the darkened, empty library he realised where they were. And how inappropriate it was.

"Lydia, what are we—"

And that's when she kissed him.

Her lips were soft against his, untutored, but full of passion. For a moment, half a second, he kissed her back and his hands flexed, wanting to pull her body into his. Then, he realised what he was doing. Christ, what the *hell* was he doing?

Pulling back, he held her from him by the shoulders. "What are you doing?"

Great hazel eyes opened, blinked slowly. She licked her lips, and he wanted to trace the path with his own tongue. Guilt bit him. She had her father's eyes. "Oliver—"

He bit back a curse, and then, fuck it, cursed anyway. "You cannot do such a thing. Is this how you behave with those boys?"

The dazed look disappeared as anger took its place. "You—"

"Do not make me tell Lord Demartine," he continued.

"Tell my father what?"

"You— I—" *Fuck.* He couldn't tell her father anything. "Your behaviour," he said lamely.

She lifted her chin. "He will not care."

"He bloody well will, if he knows his daughter throws herself at men old enough to be her—" Christ, was he really old enough to be her father? "Uncle."

She threw him a withering look. "You're not that old."

"Old enough. And you are too young. Lydia, you're barely eighteen."

"So?"

"I'm thirty-two!"

"So?"

"No. Just no. Whatever you're thinking, it can't happen."

"I'm thinking I love you," she said.

His blood chilled. "You don't know what love is."

"*Don't* tell me what I know."

"Lydia, be serious. You have not even debuted to society yet. You will meet so many people, and you will forget—"

"I *won't* forget." Her chin set mutinously. "I won't change my mind. I love you, Oliver."

He shook his head. She couldn't love him. It was a crush. Only a crush.

"You are so *obstinate*." Determination setting her jaw, she gripped his upper arms and stood on her toes. She was going to kiss him again. She was going to kiss him and he was going to have to resist. She was *eighteen*.

"Lydia!"

They both froze. Oliver didn't want to turn. He knew that voice.

"Lydia. Unhand Lord Roxwaithe." Lord Demartine said.

White-faced, Lydia stared at Oliver with wild eyes. "Papa—"

"Now, Lydia."

Averting her gaze, she stepped back.

His heart ached at the shame in her expression. He didn't want her to feel…She shouldn't feel *shame.* "Lydia—"

"Find your mother, Lydia," Lord Demartine said.

"Yes, Papa," she mumbled. Without a glance his way, she left the room.

"Oliver."

He didn't want to turn. He didn't want to see the disappointment in Lord Demartine's eyes. Eventually, he had no choice.

Lord Demartine regarded him soberly. "She is eighteen, Oliver."

"I know, sir."

"She still has a lot to experience."

"I know, sir."

"You know timing is everything?"

His brows drew. "Sir?"

Lord Demartine regarded him for the longest time. Finally, he shook his head. "It is of no concern,

Roxwaithe. Come." He held his arm out, gestured. "We have a ball to attend."

Three months later, Lydia and her mother left for the Continent. Oliver told himself he was happy for her, that he didn't require her constant presence in his life. He wouldn't miss her.

Oliver was thirty-two and three months when he knew he lied.

Chapter One

Roxegate,
London, England,
July, 1819

HE'D READ THE SAME sentence three times.

Pinching the bridge of his nose, Oliver focused on the report before him and ignored the complaints of his stomach. He'd been at his desk since seven o'clock that morning, and he'd only just realised he'd missed lunch. Par for the course, really. His staff knew not to disturb him when the study door was shut and would no doubt deliver a larger dinner to make up for the shortfall, if he remembered to make his way to the dining room. Perhaps he should take a small break and ring for a footman to deliver a sandwich or some such, but from the corner of his eye he saw the towers of reports and papers his secretary had left this morning and discarded it as the wishful thinking it was.

Exhaling, he leant his head on the back of his chair and looked out the window, resolving to ignore his stomach. Outside it was murky and grey, but when was London not murky and grey? The murky afternoon would pass into a murky evening, and then turn to a murky morning. London was nothing if not consistent. The street lamp outside the window would soon be lit, and then carriages against cobblestones would rumble past as society travelled to their amusements for the evening.

He'd remain in his study and work, as he had most evenings for the past year and a half. He couldn't remember the last time he'd attended a gathering of society, apart from the occasional dinner at Torrence House or with Wainwright and his lady. There was too much to do and there was little to tempt him to abandon it.

Without him realising, his gaze had strayed to the chair by the fireplace and the stack of books on the table beside it.

Jerking his gaze back where it belonged, Oliver leant over the report open on his desk. This one was from the steward of Waithe Hall, the usual quarterly report. He could count on one hand the number of times he'd been to Waithe Hall since becoming the earl but he'd not stayed there, instead staying at Bentley Close, the neighbouring estate owned by the Marquis of Demartine. Waithe Hall held too many ghosts.

Exhaling steadily, he glanced at the report and his gaze snagged on an odd phrase. Frowning, he reread the passage. The villagers of Waithe Village were still reporting strange lights troubling Waithe Hall, and the report claimed wild stories rioted in its wake. The villagers spoke of ghosts and ghouls, with a particular favourite being the old legend of a housekeeper of Waithe Hall roaming in search of her lost keys. He remembered as children, Alexandra and Maxim would search the hall for her keys and—

He drew in his breath. A dull ache pained him at the thought of his lost brother.

Shaking himself, he closed the report. He'd mentioned this phenomenon to Lord Demartine last month, but the earl had dismissed the report as so much talk, citing the Hall's history of ghost stories that always amounted to nothing.

His gaze again strayed to the chair opposite. Jerking it away, he focussed on a report of the Roxwaithe shipping concern. They'd come close to losing another shipment on the passage around South Africa, treacherous waters and pirates doing their utmost to inflict damage. Lord Demartine had been right in his advice, however. The employ of a master navigator and a host of security staff had taken care of both concerns. Lord Demartine often said to make money one had to spend money, and the adage had proved true once more.

Pinching the bridge of his nose again, he exhaled. At least he had no parliamentary concerns. The summer session had ended the week previous, though he would remain in London through autumn and most of winter. Perhaps in the new year he would visit the Penzance estate. Lord and Lady Demartine were due to tour the Continent, and their offspring would more than likely remove to Bentley Close in the coming months. There would be nothing in London bar work, and he could do that by the sea as well as he could do it in the capital.

The door to his study opened. "I am not ready, Rajitha," he said. "Come back in an hour."

"Roxwaithe?"

His head jerked up.

Instead of his secretary, a woman stood in the doorway. Light from the large windows in the entrance hall outlined her form and cast the rest of her in shadow. For a moment, for half a second, his heart beat faster and an inexplicable joy crashed through him. Then she stepped forward.

She wasn't as tall, and her hair was blonde instead of a reddish kind of gold. Her dress was a sensible shade of cream, and she wore a mint green spencer, the short jacket suggesting she had traversed the street between their houses rather than clamber through their shared attic.

It wasn't disappointment he felt. Of course it wouldn't be her.

Standing, he greeted Lydia's sister. "Lady Alexandra."

"Lord Roxwaithe." At his gesture, Alexandra seated herself in the chair before his. "How are you?"

"I am well." This was odd. He couldn't recall Alexandra had ever entered his study, unlike Lydia, who had burst through the door more times than he could possibly recall. "And you? Your family?"

"I and they are well. My mother asks after you and invites you to dine with us Wednesday next."

"I should be delighted to attend." It was a strange circumstance with Alexandra. He'd know her since her birth but she always brought to mind his brother. As children, she and Maxim had been joined at the hip and no matter the years that had passed since his death, the sight of Alexandra Torrence brought a deluge of memories and with them, a wave of grief. "Will it be family only?"

She nodded. "Though my middle brother is still on tour. George is in Prague. We receive letters from him on occasion, and always filled with the most excruciating details. Apparently, he has discovered a history of grotesquery in an abandoned medical clinic outside Karlin."

Oliver concealed a smile. The Torrences had always had odd interests and George, true to their nature, was obsessed with the medical and sought out grotesqueries across the Continent. "How many clinics is that now?"

"Four." Her lips twisted ruefully. "One would almost believe my brother to be searching them out rather than educating himself on history and art."

"And your other brothers?"

"They are both well. Preparations for Harry's wedding proceed, and Michael is doing well at Eton."

"I am glad to hear it."

She smiled. The fire crackled, and in the distance, he could hear the movements of his staff as they went about their duties outside the study.

"My sister is also well," Alexandra finally said.

He told himself his interest in Lydia was no different than any other who was acquainted with her. "Is she?"

"Since her return from the Continent, she has cut a broad swathe through the Ton. Papa has had to wade through all the gentlemen wishing to court her."

Dull pain lodged in his chest as he made a noncommittal noise. He was too young for heart problems. Maybe it was because he hadn't eaten.

He knew Lydia had returned. Three months ago. She'd toured Paris, Venice, and Vienna for a year and a half, and he'd braced himself for seeing her for the first time since her eighteenth birthday ball. He'd needn't have bothered as it had been, by anyone's reckoning, anticlimactic. He'd attended a family dinner at Torrence House, and his palms had sweated and his heart had raced, but when she had spied him, her gaze had slid over him with a polite smile as if there were nothing between them. As if she hadn't said she'd loved him. In the months since her return, she'd spoken all of four words to him, and only then after he'd welcomed her home. *Thank you, Lord Roxwaithe.*

"She'll be at the Fanning ball tonight," Alexandra said.

His hands curled into fists. "Along with most of London," he said as indifferently as he could. "Forgive me, Lady Alexandra, but what brings you to Roxegate?"

Sitting back in her chair, she asked, "I cannot visit an old family friend?"

"You have not done so before," he said bluntly. "How can I assist you?"

She bit her lip. "My father told me of a report. From Waithe Hall."

Of course. The Torrences had peculiar interests. Her brother was interested in medical grotesquery, her sister in tying men in knots, and Alexandra Torrence was interested in the occult.

"Father won't expand upon it, but you will, won't you, Roxwaithe?" She looked at him beseechingly.

He didn't know how to respond. At more than one house party, Alexandra searched its rooms and halls for evidence of ghostly visitation. Lord Demartine spoke with pride of the lexicon Alexandra had gathered, and encouraged his eldest daughter in her pursuits. The Torrences were, as previous, uniformly odd.

They were, however, his family. He and Stephen had leaned heavily on the Torrences when

Maxim had died, and when he'd become the earl, Lord Demartine's council had steered him from disaster too often to count. It was strange Lord Demartine did not wish to encourage Alexandra in this particular pursuit, but he would not go against the Marquis's wishes. "I am sorry, Lady Alexandra," he said quietly.

"It is only it is such an interesting circumstance, and I have a personal connection to Waithe Hall. I already know all the tales and…."

"Waithe Hall is closed, Alexandra. No doubt it is simply the villagers' imaginations."

"No doubt," she echoed. "You will tell me, though, should there be any more reports?"

"I will discuss them with your father, and relay to him any necessary impact to Bentley Close."

"That's not what I—" She sighed. "Thank you, Roxwaithe." Getting to her feet, she gave him a small smile. "I shall trouble you no further and leave you to your work."

Hastily, he rose. "It was no trouble."

She gave another smile and turned to leave.

Unable to stop himself, he said, "Your family are to the Fanning ball tonight?"

She paused, clearly surprised. He didn't blame her. "Yes. Will we see you there, my lord?"

Of course he wouldn't attend. He never attended balls anymore. "Yes," he said, surprising even himself.

A frown troubled her brow briefly. "I hope you will seek me out."

Remembering his manners, he said, "And that you shall save me a dance."

"Of course. No need to see me out," she said as he stepped from behind his desk.

He hovered awkwardly. "But—"

"We are practically family."

They were. Lord Demartine was more of a father to him than his ever had been.

"Good day, my lord." Alexandra left, closing the door quietly behind her.

Slowly, he lowered himself into his chair. He never went to balls anymore. Hell, had he even responded to the invitation?

He rang for his secretary and Rajitha was, as always, prompt in his response. "Yes, my lord?"

"Rajitha, did I respond to the Fanning invite?"

It took Rajitha but a moment to respond. "No, my lord."

"In that case, do so now in the affirmative and extend my apologies to Lady Fanning for the lateness of my reply."

"Yes, my lord. Do you require anything further?"

"Not at the moment. Thank you, Rajitha."

The secretary offered a short bow and departed.

Leaning back in his chair, Oliver stared again out the window. Why he'd agreed to go to the ball baffled him. He'd only been to a handful of gatherings in the last year; he had been busy, and he hadn't wanted to make things awkward for her. For Lydia. After the dinner where she'd ignored him, he'd barely seen her, mostly by design. She clearly had no wish to renew their friendship and he had no desire to force his presence where it wasn't wanted. She'd obviously realised her actions on her eighteenth birthday had been a mistake and if her determined pursuit of other men was any indication, she had realised all she had felt was a crush. Theirs had always been an unusual friendship, and it was always a given she would grow out of it. It was for the best, really. No doubt one day soon he would be holding the invitation to her wedding.

Belatedly, he looked down at his fist. How odd. The paper within it was crushed. Methodically, he smoothed the paper, making it line up with the others on his desk.

The ball tonight could be interesting. Perhaps he should start the search for a bride. Lydia was cutting a swathe through the Ton, perhaps he could do the same. He would be thirty-five on his next birthday and though he had Stephen as his heir, his brother also had yet to marry and set up his nursery.

He stared down at the creased paper. It would be fine to see her tonight. Maybe they would even share a dance and, maybe, they would again be friends. Maybe she would tell him of her adventures, and she would laugh and tease him as she always had, and things would be...normal.

Shaking himself, he turned back to his work. Maybe was a dangerous word. Maybe was hope and desire, and could lead to disappointment as much as anything. He would attend the ball and maybe, if he was lucky, it would be unremarkable.

Chapter Two

From the balcony, Lydia stared into darkness. Behind her, the sounds of the Fanning ball drifted into the night: laughter and music, crystal clinking and conversation. A warm breeze lifted the curls lying against her nape, playing her hair gently against her skin.

Closing her eyes, she allowed London to wash over her. She'd enjoyed her time on the Continent immensely but she'd missed the country of her birth, and now she'd returned she took every opportunity to soak in that which made England. There was nothing quite like the capital on a summer's eve, with the threat of a thunderstorm brewing in the distance and the scent of honeysuckle and lilies carried on the breeze.

"Here you are." Lord Matthew Whitton leaned one shoulder against the door jamb, a rakish smirk on his handsome face.

Placing her elbows against the balustrade, she returned his smile. All evening they'd sent each other glances and it seemed the game they'd played had now come to a head. "Here I am."

"I thought to offer you my arm and a dance, Lady Lydia."

"Did you?" Amusement filled her as he frowned, clearly not expecting such a dismissive response. However, he recovered quickly, his face once more wreathed with a rakish grin.

"I did, but I am much taken with this interaction instead," he said. "There is nothing more beautiful than a lady bathed in moonlight."

"Any lady, sir? One would think a certain specificity in this situation would be warranted."

A frown touched his brow before it smoothed again, his smile seductive. "Of course I am referring to you, Lady Lydia. There is none in London who can rival your beauty."

"Only London? Fie, I did hope for a greater reach."

Again, consternation. Inwardly, she sighed. She found her countrymen had not the skill of the French or the wit of the Viennese.

Eventually, comprehension lit his gaze that she sought to further their game. "I am covered in blushes to have been so gauche as to suggest such, my lady. I have not yet been further than our own fair country, and so did not think to compare beauties in other lands. Forgive me."

"But of course, sir. It is an easy mistake to make."

He grinned broadly. "You are quite jolly, aren't you?"

Disappointment filled her. "Lord Matthew, you do not abandon a flirtation in the middle. When you do make it to Paris and beyond, the ladies will be most disappointed."

"I have other skills."

She watched as he came closer. Raising his hand, he lifted a curl from her nape and twined it around his finger. "Shall I show you?"

"It is of supreme discourtesy to offer such a thing and then not display it."

The corner of his lip lifted. "So shall I?"

Her response was to simply raise a brow.

Slowly, he bent his head and his lips brushed hers, gentle and sweet. What would be his next move? Would he believe, because she'd agreed to a kiss, she'd agree to more? Or was he a sensible boy, and realise a woman agreeing to a kiss meant just that?

It seemed he was a sensible boy. His lips moved against hers, long dark lashes resting against his cheeks. It was so unfair. Why did men always have the beautiful lashes? Her own were stubby things, such she'd taken to darkening them with beeswax and soot as her French lady's maid had shown her in Paris.

With a sigh, Lord Matthew pulled back, his arms still caging her to the balustrade. "That was pleasant," he said softly.

It *was* pleasant. Lord Matthew was a pleasant enough fellow, and he seemed to understand the game with minimal prodding. He was at most two years her elder and the heir to the Earl of Cornell. Her family would be pleased should she announce he courted her. There was absolutely no reason she shouldn't fall in love with him.

The loud clearing of a throat interrupted them. Lord Matthew hastily pushed himself from her, his charming smile fading as he paled. Lydia couldn't fault him his reaction. The Earl of Roxwaithe in a cold temper was a terrifying sight.

Jaw clenched, Oliver stood rigid, blocking the entrance to the house. Dark brows drew further over cold grey eyes, noting Lord Matthew still stood closer to her than was proper, while full lips tightened into a displeased line. Long golden brown hair was clubbed back at his nape, and a close-cropped beard shadowed his strong jaw. An immaculately tailored coat clung to wide shoulders that tapered to narrow hips, and buff-coloured breeches covered powerful thighs. She knew, in the past, he'd spent time at Peterson's Gymnasium because whenever she had mentioned it, his cheeks would ruddy and he'd become bashful, so she'd made sure to mention it often. He was half a foot taller than she, towering over most men, and with his hands behind his back, there was little to distract from the awesome breadth of him.

Heart racing, she wet her lips. Damn him, the sight of him still made her weak.

Coldly, Oliver said, "I was unaware you knew Lady Lydia, Whitton."

"I, ah—" Throwing her a helpless glance, Lord Matthew edged toward the French doors.

Without removing her gaze from Oliver, Lydia said, "I'll see you back in the ballroom, my lord."

"Yes. Thank you," Lord Matthew bowed and departed in haste. He had to edge around Oliver, who stood his ground and watched him silently, eyes glinting in the low light.

When they were alone, she said, "Good evening, Roxwaithe. Are you enjoying the ball?"

"What were you doing with that boy?" he said without preamble.

She shrugged. "Playing."

His expression became colder. "That is your explanation?"

"I wasn't aware I had anything to explain."

"He does not even stay to protect you or ensure your safety. You chose poorly, Lydia."

She sighed. "It was a dalliance, nothing more."

"Even worse. As your elder—"

She laughed without mirth. "Oh yes, please. Do tell me as my elder what I should do."

"As your elder," he continued, as if she hadn't spoken at all. "It behoves me to warn you against playing fast and loose with your reputation."

"It is mine to do with as I please, and no concern of yours."

"Whatever occurred on the Continent, it is different in London."

"You have no notion of what occurred on the Continent."

His jaw worked. "I see," he said stiffly.

"I'm not sure you do," she retorted. Let him think the worst of her. Let. Him.

Glancing beyond her, he seemingly collected himself. "Regardless of what occurred, you are in London, amongst society. What was permissible in Paris is not here."

"Why are you saying such things to me, as if I do not know the rules? I know them as well as you."

His lips twisted. "Yes. You know them so well you allow a boy to maul you in full view of the ballroom."

"He wasn't mauling me."

"From where I stood, he was certainly mauling you."

"How, pray, was he mauling me? He had both hands on the balustrade." Damnation, but he had no right to interfere. None.

"He was caging you."

"He was not," she retorted.

"I thought he was attacking you!"

"Well, he wasn't!"

The words hung in the night air. Chest heaving, he stared at her, his grey eyes tumultuous. Her chest hurt. How was it they were yelling at each other? Where had it gone so wrong?

Oh, she remembered. When he had rejected her.

"I apologise," he said.

She turned her face away, willing the tears that burned her eyes to do the same. "Is that all you have to say?"

The gentle breeze picked again at the hair on her nape. In the distance, people laughed and music played.

"I apologise profusely," he finally said.

Bitterness twisted her lips. "Thank you for your condescension, Roxwaithe. I appreciate it greatly."

He frowned. "You're calling me Roxwaithe."

"It is your name. What else should you be called?"

Glancing away, he shrugged.

No. No, he could not do this to her. She would not feel guilty. She wouldn't. "Roxwaithe," she stressed. "Is there aught else you wish to chide me on? My gown, perhaps? The length of my bodice? Perhaps my hair is incorrectly arranged."

His expression hardened. "No. Simply the company you keep."

"Ah, something that has absolutely nothing to do with you. Well done."

He opened his mouth as if he would retort then pressed his lips together. Bowing sharply, he turned on his heel and, before she could say another word, left the balcony.

Crossing her arms, she stared after him. She wanted to storm after him, grab him and *demand* he pay her attention, but such action had never done her much good, had it? He'd decided to ignore her, and heaven forbid anyone try to change Oliver Farlisle's mind once he'd decided something. It was just like when she'd come back from the Continent. He'd avoided her until he'd been forced to greet her, and then it had been with such an air of disinterest, it had been all she could do to scrounge disinterest in return.

Digging her fingers into her biceps, she forced herself to remain where she was. She'd been so certain they were meant for each other, and the night of her eighteenth birthday had seemed the perfect occasion to show him she was ready. She'd kissed him and, inexperienced though she had been, she'd felt him respond. But then he'd pushed her from him, and the horrified look on his face had almost destroyed her.

When her father had discovered them and sent her to her mother as if she were a child, she'd been so ashamed she'd simply done as he'd commanded. Her mother had been surprised to see her, but when her father had also appeared and, after a few moments of furious whispering, promptly decamped, her mother had turned to her with a wry comprehension.

"So, your father interrupted something," her mother had said.

Pressing her lips together, Lydia hadn't responded.

"Lydia?" her mother had prompted.

Digging her fingers into her biceps, she'd stared at the floor.

Her mother had sighed. "Lydia, were you kissing Lord Roxwaithe?"

Still she hadn't answered.

"Did you kiss him or did he kiss you?"

"What does that matter?" she'd burst out.

"It matters." Her mother had waited.

"I kissed him," she'd finally admitted.

Her mother had sighed again. "I thought so." Her mother had come closer to sit beside her, taking her hand. "Lydia, you cannot force someone to feel as you do."

"I am not forcing him to feel anything. He loves me."

"As a sister—"

"No. He loves me."

Her mother had shaken her head. "Even if he does, he's not ready and you cannot force him."

"*Why* isn't he ready?" she'd asked plaintively. "He's had *years*."

"We do not all wake up at the same time, my love." Her mother had smoothed a curl behind Lydia's ear. "You are yet young, Lydia, and you've seen little of the world. You may have chosen him, but perhaps you should make sure he *is* your choice."

"What do you mean?"

"We have not been to Paris for an age. I will take you. We will shop for your wardrobe and we will attend Parisian society. Perhaps someone will catch your eye."

"No one will catch my eye," she'd said stubbornly.

"Perhaps not, but would you not rather know for sure?"

Exhaling, Lydia rested her forehead on her arms folded on the balustrade. The next day, she'd gone to his study. It had taken every scrap of courage she'd possessed, but she'd resolved to act as if nothing had happened. She could wait. She'd been patient for eighteen years, she could wait a few months more until he came to realise she was a woman grown. However, his study had been locked. She'd stood there dumbly and she'd tried the handle again and it still wouldn't turn. In a daze, she'd returned home. Four days later, she'd been on a ship bound for Paris.

Lydia had done her best to allow someone to catch her eye. She'd been merry and she'd flirted, she'd kissed others and managed to garner a marriage proposal or three. She'd thrown herself into gaiety, pretending she was carefree and her heart had not been claimed before she'd even known what it meant.

Cursing under her breath, she tried to recapture the calm the night afforded her. Damn him. Damn him for destroying her peace. Why could she not rid herself of this? Everyone claimed it was a silly crush. Everyone said she would forget him, that she would fall in love a dozen times before settling on a man to wed. Her friends fell in love with alarming frequency, and each ball offered a new suitor. Why was it she couldn't do the same?

But then...no one else had ever caught her eye.

Using the heels of her hands, she wiped her eyes and, pinching her cheeks, she forced a smile as she left the balcony.

The ball still whirled, even more people adding to its crush. She pushed through the crowd, smiling and laughing and greeting those she knew.

"There you are!" In a cloud of frills and perfume, Lady Violet Crafers appeared at her side. "Lord Seebohm has been asking after you, and Mr Harris was determined to claim his dance."

"I apologise I was not present." She'd missed Violet while she was away. Violet could, and had, filled reams of paper with every *on dit* she came across, but it wasn't the same as watching her friend wildly gesticulate as she reported the latest gossip.

Violet's smile turned sly. "I saw Lord Matthew Whitton follow you."

"Did you?" she said diffidently, knowing it would drive her friend wild.

Violet whacked her with her fan. "Do not give me that. He followed you. What happened?"

Lydia smiled mysteriously.

Violet whacked her with her fan again, her dark curls bobbing. "I knew it! You are a wicked bad woman, Lydia."

"Perhaps, but I am also a woman who knows how Lord Matthew kisses," she said archly.

Violet sucked in her breath. "And?" she asked breathlessly.

"I shouldn't repeat the experience." She deliberately didn't think of the events that followed.

Violet's face fell. "That is disappointing. I always thought he would be good at it."

Lydia shrugged.

"Oh well." Violet smiled sunnily. "Shall we see what refreshments are yet available?"

As they walked from the ballroom and to the refreshment room, Violet chatted steadily, reporting every piece of gossip she'd heard over the last few days. Lydia listened, glad of the distraction. She would not let Oliver ruin her evening. She was here to have fun and by god, fun she would have.

Violet slowed as they approached the refreshments. "Oh," she said in consternation.

"What is it?" Lydia followed her line of sight. Standing at the refreshments, sipping from a crystal glass, stood Seraphina Waller-Mitchell. "Oh."

Violet's lips turned down. "I do not wish to deal with her this evening."

No one in their right mind wished to deal with Seraphina Waller-Mitchell. Seraphina looked down her nose at everyone, whether they were princess or scullery maid or any permutation in between. They were all plebeians to her, and unworthy of her time.

She had, however, decided Lydia was worth her time. At some stage, Lydia had incurred her wrath and she had dedicated herself to singling Lydia out at every occasion. Lydia had no idea why. Seraphina was six years her elder and thus Lydia should have been beneath her notice, yet Seraphina had gone out of her way to make comment on her choice of gown, how she styled her hair, her dancing companion, the way she held her head. Seraphina had an opinion on it all, and all of it snide.

Tonight, Seraphina stood with a punch glass in her hand, her chin arrogantly high as she surveyed the room. Her henchwomen, Maria Spencer and Elizabeth Harcourt, flanked her, the three of them ready to attack whoever was foolish enough to stray near them.

Lydia squared her shoulders. "Come," she said to Violet.

Violet wet her lips. "Do we have to?"

"Do not worry. I will protect you."

A little green, Violet followed as Lydia strode for the refreshment table.

Seraphina Waller-Mitchell smiled at them. "Lady Lydia. Lady Violet. *Such* a delight to see you. And in such...gowns."

How Seraphina Waller-Mitchell turned a smile into an insult was truly a work of art. "And you, Lady Seraphina." Lydia forced herself to say no more, instead picking up a plate and helping herself to a sandwich triangle.

Seraphina watched her with interest while Maria Spencer and Elizabeth Harcourt glared, obviously waiting for Seraphina's direction.

Lydia ignored them, piling sandwich after sandwich onto her plate. She refused to be intimidated, she absolutely refused. The back of her neck prickled, and she ignored the coldness slithering down her spine.

"How are Lord Henry's wedding preparations proceeding?" Seraphina asked suddenly.

"Well," she replied cautiously.

"I am so pleased to hear that."

She wasn't going to ask. This was how Seraphina drew you in. She made a statement and then—

Seraphina smiled thinly. "I knew there was nothing to the rumours."

Don't ask, don't ask, don't—

"What rumours?" Violet asked, and immediately looked to be castigating herself for responding.

"You've not heard the rumours?" Seraphina asked, her tone arch. Maria Spencer exchanged a knowing look with Elizabeth Harcourt, who simply smirked.

Lydia grit her teeth. This was what Seraphina did, she reminded herself. She cast doubt with baseless rumour.

Seraphina's expression brimmed with false sympathy. "I am certain there is nothing in them, absolutely certain."

"There is nothing wrong with Harry and Tessa," Violet burst out.

Silently, Lydia regarded Seraphina.

The other woman met her gaze, the corners of her lips lifting slightly. "No. Of course not. Nothing at all."

Maria and Elizabeth watched breathlessly while Lydia held Seraphina's gaze, refusing to yield to the woman.

"I'll bid you good evening, Lady Seraphina. I do hope you enjoy the ball," Lydia finally said, as calmly as she could manage.

"I shall, Lady Lydia. You may rely upon it." Seraphina said with a smile that would slice one so precisely, one wouldn't realise one bled until five paces away.

Taking Violet's elbow, Lydia led them away. Her skin thrummed, and she wanted quite illogically to smash something.

"Oh, I wish I could just slap that smirk off her face," Violet seethed.

"I know, but we can't. She's horrible, Violet. Don't think on her any longer."

"It's a lie, you know."

"I know."

"Whatever she's heard, it's a lie."

"Most likely she's fishing, or attempting to stir contrary where there is none. I shouldn't think on it, Violet."

"No."

But they both knew they would. "In any event," Lydia said, "Harry would tell us if there was a worry."

Violet gave her a look. "Lydia," she said. "Harry is a man."

"True," she conceded. "Tessa would tell us. Rumours are not facts, Violet. We should not treat them as if they were."

Violet exhaled. "She just makes me so mad."

She rubbed her friend's arm comfortingly. "Let us enjoy the rest of the ball. We shan't let her taint our evening."

"Agreed." Violet determinedly popped a sandwich in her mouth.

"Who shall we allow to dance with us, do you think?"

A reluctant smile tilted her friend's lips. "Only the most handsome and the most intelligent."

"Both? That will narrow the field considerably." Lydia's gaze wandered over the throng. Oliver was not among them. Most likely he was in the card room with his friend Wainwright. It was how he usually spent his time at a ball and—

She closed her eyes, annoyed at herself. Taking a breath, she forced a smile and, with Violet at her side, she entered the fray.

Chapter Three

OLIVER STARED DOWN AT his cards, but for the life of him, he could not concentrate. His mind was on a balcony and the pale face of a woman he hadn't truly spoken with in nearly two years.

"I say, are you well, man?" Cards held loosely in his hand, Wainwright regarded him with furrowed brow.

"I'm fine," he said, even as he again saw the hurt on Lydia's face.

"I think Wainwright's correct." Her own cards ignored, Lady Wainwright peered at Oliver. "You do appear decidedly peaked."

"I promise I'm fine." Shifting in his seat, he concentrated on the cards in his hand.

"Don't tease him, Lady Wainwright," Wainwright said. "He has managed to emerge once again into society, much like a newly born chick hatching and blinking eyes at a bright and terrible world. We shouldn't discourage him."

Lady Wainwright nodded gravely. "It is true. We should encourage his brave venture into the unknown."

"It must be confusing, being amongst other people," Wainwright continued. "Why, look how he retreats to those he knows rather than enjoy the charms of strangers in his midst."

"Yes, it is odd. For two years, we have noted his presence at only the occasional society outing, and even then I do not recall seeing him at a *ball* for well over a year. What, pray tell, could have changed?"

"I have no notion, my dear. Shall we ask him?"

"Yes, let us ask him." They both turned overly expectant expressions to him.

Exhaling, Oliver scowled at his cards. Wainwright was barely concealing his glee, his light blue eyes alight. His lady held the same expression, her own cornflower blue gaze trained with false innocence upon him. He'd known Wainwright since his first year at Eton and, as his closest friend, Wainwright's favourite sport was to needle Oliver, though to be fair Oliver's favourite sport was to needle his friend back. When his friend had wooed and wed the girl who would become Lady Wainwright, he'd thought perhaps marriage would put a halt to their sport. Instead, Lady Wainwright had valiantly entered the playing field and now he had two people who delighted in needling him. "Are you done?"

"I don't know. My dear, are we done?" Wainwright asked his lady.

"I'm unsure, Wainwright. He has not yet answered our question."

"You didn't ask a question, you issued a statement," Oliver pointed out, but when had logic ever stopped Wainwright and his lady?

"True, true. How very remiss of us." Lady Wainwright propped her chin in her hand. "What has changed?"

Christ. One would have thought he would have learnt by now. He cast a desperate look at Wainwright, but his friend merely grinned maniacally. "I simply felt the need for society."

"How odd. Society. And yet he has not felt the need for— How long was it again, dear?"

"Almost two years," Wainwright answered, an unholy gleam to his eye.

"Almost two whole years. My. One might suppose something in particular has prompted this re-emergence. Is it something in particular, Roxwaithe?"

Oliver cast his gaze toward the refreshment room. "Has not Miss Hurcombe taken an age? Perhaps she requires assistance."

"My sister is capable of returning from the refreshments by herself." Lady Wainwright's lips twitched. "Do tell us what has changed, Roxwaithe."

"I told you. I had a strange need for society, which I am now regretting."

Wainwright propped his elbow on the back of his chair. "My dear, do you think he means us?" he said to his wife.

"I rather think he does," she responded brightly.

"I rue the day I met you," Oliver told Wainwright.

"Alas, we were but young lads then, and Eton held enough horrors that we are forever bound to one another. We will stop now, though," Wainwright said magnanimously, waving his hand in the air.

"Thank you ever so," Oliver said.

Lady Wainwright stood. "Actually, Cynthia *has* been an age. I should go see what is keeping her."

Passing a brief caress over her husband's shoulder, she abandoned them for the refreshments room.

Oliver watched her go before turning back to his cards only to catch Wainwright regarding him closely. "What?"

"There is truth in our jests, you know. You rarely attend balls anymore."

"You rarely attend either."

"Ah, but we have children and an estate in Penrith."

"I have an estate in Northumberland."

"You are never there, whereas we spend most of the year in Penrith. In fact, we return next week."

"You will? You did not tell me."

"It is hard to tell a person anything when one does not see them."

"We saw each other in Hyde Park two weeks ago."

"'Saw each other' being the operative. You lurked in the shrubbery and scowled at every passerby. We did not speak."

"I don't lurk in shrubbery."

Wainwright raised a brow.

"Fine, it must have been…." Oliver racked his brain. Belatedly, he remembered dining with Wainwright at their club a month ago. Had it really been that long?

Wainwright smirked.

Oliver exhaled. "I concede, it has been a while. When next week will you depart?"

"Tuesday. Lady Wainwright has a commitment that prevents us from leaving before then. We know why, anyway."

"Know what?"

"Why you are here. Lydia Torrence is looking decidedly well this evening."

Heat rose from his neck and, of a sudden, his cards were of intense interest.

"It is strange how she has returned from the Continent to enter London society and now you have deigned to attend a ball. What's next?" Wainwright continued. "Will Lady Wainwright and I see you at the theatre next week?"

"No, you're departing London next week," he said sourly.

"The *theatre*, Roxwaithe," Wainwright continued blithely. "And yet, you do not approach her. What happened? There was a time when you could not speak but to mention her."

His head whipped up. "Pardon?"

"Every second word was an observation of Lydia Torrence's. Lady Wainwright was convinced you would offer for her as soon as she made her bow."

He stared at his friend in disbelief. "She is fourteen years younger than me."

"So?"

"She is a *child*."

Wainwright opened his mouth to respond only to look past him. "She doesn't look like a child," he said.

Brows drawn, he followed Wainwright's gaze. Lydia had entered the room, glorious in a gown of soft green and pale gold, and the low-cut bodice made it obvious to all that she was not a child. Not in the slightest. The group of young men surrounding her followed her to a card table, fawning over her as she took her seat.

During the year and more she'd been away, she'd grown fully into her looks, becoming a woman for all he protested otherwise. Her upswept red-gold hair rioted around features that fulfilled the promise of beauty, a straight nose and high cheekbones framing a mouth with a thin upper lip and a full lower one. She'd done something to them and they were redder than he remembered, glistening in the candlelight and making him want to slick them with his own tongue.

Christ, what was he thinking? Hastily, he averted his gaze.

"A child, is she?" Wainwright asked.

Oliver didn't respond.

"She is nineteen, is she not?"

"Twenty."

"Twenty. Then, I would hypothesise she is not, as you say, a child."

"She is still too young."

Wainwright studied him. "If you say so."

"Besides, she is as a sister to me," Oliver felt compelled to add. "She and Lady Alexandra both. All the Torrences are as family, and Lord Demartine has always assisted me greatly with the management of the Roxwaithe estate. Perhaps that is why I spoke of her often."

"Perhaps."

"I enjoyed her company when she was growing, but she is in society now. She had that time on the Continent, which I can only think was for the best. Look how popular she has become."

"A veritable Incomparable."

"Yes. I imagine Lord Demartine is inundated with requests for permission to court her." The words tasted bitter. "I saw her on the balcony with Whitton," he said abruptly.

For a moment, all was silent. He refused to look at Wainwright, refused to see what might be in Wainwright's gaze. "Did you?"

"I yelled at her. I have not spoken with her for an age and I—" His voice cracked. Swallowing, he again saw her pale face, the anger, the hurt. "I yelled at her," he repeated softly.

"What were they doing?" Wainwright asked. "She and Whitton?"

"They— He—" Bile rose in his throat.

"Ah." Wainwright paused. "Do you truly believe she is like a sister?"

He stared down at his clenched fist, the cards bending in his grip. "Yes."

"Then you have no say. She makes her own decisions. Unless you give her a reason to change her mind, you cannot interfere."

"What if she is behaving recklessly with her reputation? You did not see them, Wainwright."

"I would wager Lady Lydia had everything well in hand."

The cards blurred. Wainwright spoke truly. Lydia always had everything well in hand.

"You cannot wait, Roxwaithe," Wainwright said, compassion stark in his tone. "She is surrounded by suitors. You will wake up one day and discover her affianced, and then married. Do not live with regret, my friend. It makes a poor bedfellow."

Oliver shook his head. His friend had no idea of what he spoke.

Wainwright sighed. "I tried," he said to the heavens.

"Tried what?" Lady Wainwright took her seat next to her husband.

"Tried to change Roxwaithe's mind. A feat doomed to failure." He looked at the empty seat beside his lady. "Where is Miss Hurcombe, my dear?"

"Cynthia was asked to dance."

"Ah." Turning his gaze, Wainwright studied Oliver.

"What?" he asked.

"You are like a woolly mammoth. When are you going to shave? I can lend you my valet, should your own be subpar."

Lady Wainwright walked her fingers up her husband's arm. "I wouldn't be so quick to remove it. I find all that hair...affecting."

Wainwright's eyes brightened. "Really? Well, my lady, shall we talk about that some?"

Oliver studied the ceiling as Wainwright and his lady flirted outrageously. He often told himself he wasn't jealous of his friend, but every now and then, envy snuck up on him. A wife who loved him, joyous children who bestowed hugs and kisses even on their hairy uncle Roxwaithe, a life that was shared....

Across the room, Lydia played her cards, laughing as she folded her hand and batted her fan on the forearm of the gentleman beside her.

Sometimes, envy snuck up on him.

Chapter Four

STANDING IN THE DOORWAY of her sister's bedchamber, Lydia said suddenly, "What are you doing?"

Alexandra jumped. "Good god!"

Grinning, Lydia entered the room. Complexion unnaturally pale, her sister still held her hand to her chest. Hmm. Maybe she had been a little too enthusiastic in her approach. "What are you doing?"

"What does it look like I'm doing?" Still scowling, Alexandra picked up a—perhaps a fichu—off her bed.

Lydia's gaze drifted over the assorted clothing scattered over the covers. "It looks a lot like packing. Why are you packing? You must be going somewhere. Where are you going?"

Alexandra folded the…Lydia was fairly certain it was a fichu. "I don't see how it's any of your business."

"Where are you going?" she repeated.

"Why must you be so annoying? I told Mama I wanted a sister after she and Papa burdened me with two brothers. More fool me."

"Where?" she demanded.

Alexandra shot her a gloriously disgruntled look. "Northumberland."

Northumberland? Their family's ancestral estate was in Northumberland. "Why are you going to Bentley Close?"

"No reason. *Don't* tell Papa."

How interesting. "Don't tell Papa what? That you are travelling or that it is to Bentley Close?"

"You know, I enjoyed it when you were on the Continent."

Lydia smirked. "Don't tell Papa what?"

"That I'm going to investigate a possible ghostly sighting at Waithe Hall," Alexandra gave in.

Lydia folded her arms. Her sister studiously continued to pack, avoiding her gaze. "Why wouldn't you want Papa to know that?" she said slowly.

Alexandra's breath exploded. "Because it is none of his concern. I am a grown woman with wealth of my own from our aunt, thus my movements are my own. If I wish to visit Bentley Close, I shall. I am allowed to travel between our estates."

"You are," Lydia agreed.

"I am allowed to investigate the spiritual as well."

"I didn't say anything to the contrary." She watched Alexandra rather aggressively continue to fold garments. "When are you leaving?"

"Tomorrow," she said, shoving something that might have been a chemise into a bag.

"I *suppose* I can avoid him until after you leave."

"Thank you ever so." Quite obviously resolving to ignore her, Alexandra continued to pack.

She watched her sister silently. Alexandra's hobby of spiritual investigation was an odd one, but it was also fascinating. Their parents were mostly indulgent of her interest, and Oliver had spoken of her father's pride in their discussions on the subject, especially when Alexandra had come tantalisingly close to getting a paper published with the Spiritual Society of North London. In any event, her interest was no less strange than George's obsession with the medical, grotesqueries in particular. And if she were pushed, she could admit her own interest in ancient architecture and urban planning was not within the normal interests of young women. Actually, her family was really quite odd when she thought about it.

Picking up the cricket ball that usually resided on Alexandra's dresser from the bed, she began tossing it in the air. "What about Mama?"

"What *about* Mama?" Noticing Lydia was handling the ball, a shadow passed over Alexandra's face. "Please be careful with that."

Moving the ball between her hands, she said, "Are you going to tell her you're going to Bentley Close?"

"No, and I don't have to. Mama is distracted by Harry's wedding. She won't even notice I'm gone." Her sister's gaze followed the movement of the ball.

"I wouldn't go that far. I would say she will notice when you don't attend the breakfast table three days in a row."

"Ah, but in three days, I'll be almost at Bentley Close." As if unable to help herself, Alexandra snatched the ball from Lydia's hands.

Curling her fingers, she watched as her sister carefully placed the cricket ball back on her dresser. "How are you travelling?"

"Stagecoach." Alexandra gave the ball a final pat before returning to her packing.

"Stagecoach? Alexandra, you should at least take the family coach—"

"I shall have my maid, and there's no call to engage staff that are not required. I shall only be there a few days. No sense rousing the grooms and farriers and coachmen just for a few days."

"Alexandra—"

"It will be safe. You can remain here and continue to cut a swathe through the male population of London without worrying about me, though I do not know why you are cutting this swathe." Frowning at another chemise, she said, "What happened to your plan of marrying Roxwaithe?"

Lydia froze. She couldn't— She— "I—I grew to realise it the fancies of a girl."

Alexandra frowned. "Fancies? It's all you've spoken of since...I cannot remember."

"Well, it *was* the fancies of a young girl. The Continent taught me much." Saucily, she smirked and ignored her heart set to pound right out her chest. "What is to be investigated at Waithe Hall?"

Alexandra's expression brightened. "The villages are reporting strange lights. Papa and Roxwaithe think it to be nothing, but it could be some sort of paranormal activity. There is so much lore surrounding Waithe Hall, more than most houses I've investigated. Did you know a woman walked to her death from a parapet about a century ago?"

Thanking her lucky stars Alexandra was so easily distracted, she said, "Good god, Alexandra, that's macabre."

"That's not the best bit," she continued, her eyes alight. "A few years later, there were reports of a woman walking the roof only to disappear. There was that story, you know, about the housekeeper forever doomed to search for keys lost. Perhaps these lights are in fact her."

"Or perhaps it is squatters trespassing on Roxwaithe property."

"Either way, I shall find out." Alexandra patted the clothes she had placed in the trunk. "Is that why you don't visit Roxegate anymore? Because you have decided you do not want to marry him after all? You used to practically live there."

It was the abrupt change in subject that set her heart to race once more, or perhaps it had never stopped. Nothing more. "I did not."

"You did. You were always over there. We only saw you for breakfast and occasionally dinner."

"That's an exaggeration."

"Not much of one." Alexandra studied her. "Did something happen?"

Lydia willed her features still. "No."

"Are you sure?"

"Of course I'm sure. Are you saying I don't know my own mind?"

"No. It's just odd, is all. You and Mama swept off to the Continent with barely a word. Mama returned, but you remained for almost two years. You've been back for three months, we haven't really talked, and now you tell me your insistence you would marry Roxwaithe as soon as you were old enough was merely a fancy."

"Justina Westhoffe invited me to stay with her family. I could not say no, especially when it meant staying longer in *Paris*. Besides, we never talked before I went away. Why would we do so now?"

Alexandra lifted a shoulder. "I had hoped perhaps we could be closer."

"Is that why you have not broached this subject until you are literally leaving for Bentley Close?"

Instead of answering, Alexandra studied her.

Lydia exhaled forcefully. "What now?"

Alexandra shook her head. "Nothing. I did not see you much at the Fanning ball."

Honestly, her sister's lightning change of subject was enough to give one whiplash. "That's because you were squirreled in the corner, probably discussing spirits or the occult or whatever it is you discuss with those paranormal people with whom you like to associate."

"You were not on the dance floor."

"I felt more like cards and conversation."

Staring at her half-packed trunk, Alexandra said absently, "Roxwaithe asked after you."

Her chest tightened. "Oh? When?"

"When I saw him yesterday. He wished to know your movements." Alexandra frowned at a petticoat. "I think I am packing too much. Do you think I am packing too much?"

"Probably. It's quite a lot for only a few days" She paused. "Why did Roxwaithe wish to know my movements?" she asked as casually as she could.

"He always asks of you." Alexandra's brows drew further. "Perhaps it will be longer than a few days I am away. Maybe a fortnight?"

"What do you mean, he always asks after me?"

"Oh, you know, while you were away. He would always ask about everyone in the family, but he would pay particular attention to any discussion involving you."

"He did?" Lydia kept her expression politely inquiring, as if what Alexandra had next to say was not of vital importance. "He never wrote me."

"Well, that would not be appropriate, would it? He is not related to us, for all we were children together: he, Stephen and—" Her voice broke. "Maxim," she finished softly.

Oliver's brother, the one who had died. Lydia remembered the funeral, how sad everyone had been. She remembered standing beside Oliver and watching as person after person offered their condolences, as his jaw became tighter and tighter. Alexandra had been grief-stricken for months, locking herself in her room to emerge for meals only, sombre and pale-cheeked.

"Why are you calling him Roxwaithe?"

Lydia blinked. Another lightning-fast subject change. "Excuse me?"

"You never call him Roxwaithe. It's always 'Oliver' this, and 'Oliver' that."

"It is his name. His title. I am no longer a girl; I should refer to people as is proper."

"You always did, but not him. What has happened?" Alexandra's gaze sharpened. "And you never said why you went to the Continent."

Heat rose in her cheeks. "Yes, I did. It was for my trousseau."

"What trousseau? You were not, and still aren't, engaged."

Her cheeks felt as if they were ablaze. "It was Mama's idea. Ask her."

Alexandra looked in no way convinced.

"Where do you want me to tell Papa you went?" she said hastily.

Alexandra pressed her lips together. "Tell him I went to Bentley Close," she finally said. "However, perhaps wait three days before telling him."

Nodding, Lydia rose from the bed and edged towards the door. "I will."

"Lydia, about Oliver—"

She stumbled in her haste. "I'll leave you to it, shall I?"

"Lydia—"

"I won't tell Papa. Have a good journey." Rushing through the door, she fled to her room and, closing her bedroom door behind her, sagged against it. Everything always circled back to Oliver.

Moving further into her room, she stared out her window. Her bedchamber looked out on the shared garden, and she knew it to be the same view he saw from his bedchamber. Cupping her elbows, she leant her forehead against the window pane. She remembered him again as he'd been last night; his brows drawn over grey eyes, his strong jaw clenched, his wide shoulders tense.

She couldn't be so wholly wrong. All her life, she'd know they would be married. Perhaps she had been too young, but the Continent had given her polish, had introduced her to other experiences and, yes, other men. Now that she'd returned, now she was older and wiser, many seemed overjoyed to have her attention, to engage in flirtation, to desire her kiss. Many, but not him.

Turning her back on the window, she looked around her bedchamber. It all seemed foreign to her. It had last been decorated when she was fourteen and obsessed with green. She had thought to one day decorate Roxegate in the same colours, but to do that, she would have need to be Oliver's countess and he, stubbornly, insisted it would not happen.

Laying down, she stared at the canopy above her bed and, quite deliberately, resolved to think of nothing. And, mostly, she did.

Chapter Five

FINGERS SPEARED THROUGH HIS hair to brace his head, Oliver scratched yet another amendment to the document before him. His eyes felt sandy and swollen, his brain muzzy, and he was desperate for sleep, but there was too much to do. It had been another long day after an even longer night. He hadn't returned to Roxegate until the early hours of the morning, and it appeared in his year or more of rustication, he'd lost the knack of burning the candle at both ends.

The quiet snick of the study door heralded Rajitha's entry. Heel of his hand pressing into his forehead, Oliver continued to work on the report before him, knowing his secretary would wait silently. It would not be anyone else. After the Fanning ball, the faint hope it might be Lydia was all but gone.

"What is it, Rajitha?" he finally asked.

"Your secretary is still in his office."

Surprise jerked his head up. Of all the people who could have entered his office, he would never have expected it to be his brother.

Stephen lowered himself into the seat opposite, his expression carefully blank. His brother was a rangy fellow, a leanness contradictory to Oliver's own more solid build. His deep-set eyes were the same grey as Oliver's but his hair was blond and his cheekbones boarded on sharpness. They looked like each other except when they didn't. Perhaps Maxim would have bridged the gap. If he had lived.

"What brings you to Roxegate, brother?" It had been a good six months since he'd last seen Stephen, and then it had been at a dinner hosted at Torrence House. Before Lydia had returned.

"I am here to beg for funds." Stephen's expression remained impassive.

"You do not have to beg for funds." Christ, his brother made him out to be a cruel fiend, jealously holding the purse strings and making him beg for the smallest of crumbs. He did no such thing. He was judicious in the release of funds, because Stephen too often sought to waste his. Their mother had left each of them funds independent of Roxwaithe, and Stephen had burned through his by the time he was twenty-five. Oliver would not allow him to do the same with what the Roxwaithe estate gave him.

Stephen's eyes hardened. "I should like funds to allow for the continued study of the mythic."

Oliver blinked. "I beg your pardon?" he finally said.

"The mythic. The spiritual. That is what Alexandra calls it, isn't it? You know. Ghosts and such." He smiled thinly.

"The spiritual." Oliver shook himself, but it still made no sense. "You wish to study the spiritual?"

"As I said."

"Since when?"

"Since when what?"

Oliver gritted his teeth. "When did this interest begin?"

"I have always possessed an interest."

"Not that I have observed. You were more likely to be outside occupying yourself with some sort of ball sport than traipsing through halls with Alexandra and Maxim hunting ghosts."

"And if Lord Roxwaithe didn't see it, then it must not have happened?"

"No, I—" Oliver exhaled. "I did not mean it such. It is a surprise. What do you require the funds for?"

"For my studies."

"Yes, I understand, but what specifically? Is there equipment that must be purchased? Dues to be paid? Are you looking for further study? Where, exactly, does one study the spiritual?" He frowned. "I do not recall Lord Demartine mentioning Alexandra petitioning him to fund her interest."

Stephen scowled. "I should have known you would not help."

Irritation nipped at Oliver. "I did not say that. It is good practice to ask these questions."

"It is because I come to you with the study of the spiritual, isn't it? If it were an investment or a charity, you would have no concern."

"That is not true, Stephen. You—"

"These funds are mine. They have been invested on my behalf. I am entitled to them."

God damn, his brother could be— Letting out a controlled breath, Oliver counted to ten. "I am the trustee and I would be remiss in my duty if I did not question what you will do with these funds. You have announced this interest out of the blue and you give no basis for the release of funds. You have not given any evidence you have done even a cursory exam."

Sullenness soured his brother's expression. "You are being unreasonable."

Oliver's temper snapped. "It is unfortunate, then, that you must seek the permission of an unreasonable man. Demonstrate when you first displayed this interest."

"As I've said. Always. I cannot remember when it began."

"Then what am I to think, brother? Or is this like the time you wanted to run Excott Manor?"

Stephen looked to the side, a muscle ticking in his jaw.

"Or when you wished to oversee the shipping concern. Or when you studied botany. Or when you thought a life of academia would suit. You tried all these things, and none of them suited. There is nothing about this latest endeavour that makes me believe it will be any different. You have approached me with an idea, not a proposal. I have nothing against ideas, Stephen, but substance is required. Reports. Evidence. Christ, the reason you are even interested. You have offered none of these."

Staring to the side, Stephen's jaw tensed. "Then, there is nothing more to say."

"There is more. Bring me the evidence. A plan. Show these funds will not be wasted. I do not wish to keep you from pursuing your interests, but there has to be some basis."

Stephen's lips twisted. "And there it is. You believe me frivolous."

Oliver cursed. "Stephen—"

Stephen stood, executing a stiff bow. "I shall bother you no longer. Good afternoon, Roxwaithe."

"Brother, do not—" But Stephen had already left, wrenching the door shut behind him.

Oliver sank back into his chair. Bloody hell. Bloody goddamned hell. Every bloody time, a discussion ended in a war between them. He did not know when this animosity had started, but it grew worse each year. Stephen would be sullen and defensive, Oliver would respond with highhandedness, and so the cycle continued.

He palmed the knot of his hair at his nape. Why could Stephen not see he only had his best interests at heart?

His gaze centred on her chair, the books stacked high beside it. He missed her. If she were here, if she still sat in that chair, he would have paced and pulled at his hair and she— A smile tugged at him. He could just see her sitting there, rolling her eyes at his dramatics and arguing him into a good mood.

His smile faded. He had acted poorly at the Fanning ball; he didn't need her to tell him that. This distance between them had to end. He would rather she was in his life than suffer the lack of her. He could keep his opinions on her amorous pursuits to himself. She wished to win herself a husband and he would not stand in her way. He was only grateful her sights were no longer set on him and they could resume their friendship. Those young men would court her and flatter her, and she would turn her smiles and attention to them. She would turn her love to them.

Brows drawn, he stared at the report before him. Lydia. Her attention on the man she would marry. Her smile for him. Her counsel for him. Her love for him.

Exhaling, Oliver pinched the bridge of his nose. And that was good. That was right.

Chapter Six

CASTING HER GAZE ABOUT the room, Lydia tapped her fan against her thigh. Most spines contained scrawled names, though in all honesty she wasn't looking forward to the commencement of the dancing. This assembly was like the dozens of others she had attended this year alone, but she felt off tonight and would have much preferred to be alone in her room. However, she had a social obligation—to her mother, her father, and her family—to attend every social gathering and be merry. Ugh. She *would* be merry. Even if it killed her.

"Isn't this amazing?" Violet gushed beside her, her foot tapping in time with the music from the ensemble.

"Yes. Of course." Good Lord, she would fool no one if she spoke in such a flat tone.

Without losing her smile, Violet made a face. "Don't be sullen, Lydia. You shan't attract a suitor if you are sullen."

"I shall," she said. Merrily. Even if it killed her. "It will just be those of a particular bent."

"Those of a particular bent *are* the most interesting. Perhaps this strategy should be adopted by all us debutantes."

"Perhaps."

Violet's breath exploded. "Honestly, Lydia, you are no fun tonight. I made what was clearly a superior jest and you completely ignore it. Whatever is the matter?"

"Nothing." Her friend looked unconvinced. "There is nothing the matter, Violet. Surely there is something more interesting for us to talk about than my potential suitors."

"I suppose we could discuss the latest *on dit*."

"Yes. Let us do that. Tell me all of the latest *on dit*. I have been on the Continent, you know."

"You've been home for months, Lydia."

"Nevertheless, all my gossip is of the Continent. Spill, Violet. I can see you are fair to bursting."

"Well...." Violet leant closer. "Did you hear about Brianna Thompson?"

"What about Brianna Thompson?"

"She was found in a compromising position with Marcus Dormer."

"Define compromising."

"They were embracing and her bodice was undone."

"Violet," she said in exasperation. The likelihood of that happening was zero. Marcus Dormer was as proper as they came, and the mere thought of him in a compromising position was absurd.

"It was shocking by all accounts, absolutely shocking."

Lydia rolled her eyes. "I heard they were standing next to each other, chatting calmly about the weather."

Violet pouted. "You are no fun. How can we gossip if you insist on being factual?"

Unconcerned, Lydia lifted a shoulder and idly surveyed the crowd.

Violet's pout faded. "Don't look."

"Why?" She followed Violet's gaze. Oh.

Oliver had entered the ballroom. He was almost painfully handsome, dressed in a sober coat and breeches, his hair fastened tightly in a knot at the base of his head.

Jerking her gaze away, she tried to calm the pounding in her chest.

"I told you not to look," Violet said.

Scowling, she said, "When, in the history of ever, has a person not looked?"

"Fair point. *Lydia, don't look, the Earl of Roxwaithe is here*," she said lamely. Sighing, she cocked her head. "Why do you like him, anyway? He is old."

"He is not old. He is older. There is a difference."

"Old. Older. In any case, he's only passably attractive. He has all that hair." Violet waved a hand.

"He's allowed to have hair." She loved his hair. Many was the time she'd stare at it, at the way he'd mess up the neatly gathered strands his valet had arranged in an approximation of a queue. She'd look at those loosely gathered strands and want—so much—to run her fingers through them....

"*And* a beard. A beard, Lydia! He's a veritable bear of a man. So common." Violet shuddered delicately.

Lydia regarded her friend suspiciously. "Are you funning me?"

"I? Fun you? Why I should never! Lydia Torrence, I do not know where you get your ideas from."

"You are funning me," she said in resignation, setting Violet off into peals of laughter.

Sobering, Violet offered, "He *does* have a lot of hair."

Lifting her chin, she refused to answer.

Of a sudden, Violet's grin vanished. "*He's* coming over," she said flatly.

All at once, a myriad of emotions assaulted Lydia—excitement, apprehension, anger. Deliberately, she kept her gaze from him, debating the best way to react. She would not allow him to berate her again. She would be polite and distant, and she would not think him the most handsome man she'd ever seen.

Pasting a wide smile on her face, she looked up—only to find the Duke of Meacham before them. A mix of disappointment and relief filled her. Disappointment it wasn't Oliver. *Relief* it wasn't Oliver.

"Lady Violet, Lady Lydia." His Grace bowed deeply over each of their hands. The Duke of Meacham was by anyone's standards in contention for the most beautiful man one had ever beheld. Dark brown hair waved back from a wide forehead boasting thick, winged brows over deep blue eyes. His nose was bold, balanced by high cheekbones, a strong jaw and full lips. His physique was athletic and his clothing perfectly flattered his form, fashionable and just this side of daring. He was very much fun to look at.

"Duke," Violet said, her tone decidedly chilly.

Lydia glanced at her friend. Arms crossed, Violet wore a scowl as she glared at the duke. Usually, Violet was swayed by a pretty face but, apparently, not the duke's pretty face.

An unholy gleam lit his painfully blue gaze as the duke absorbed her ire, lending him a saturnine air that, somehow, made him even more attractive.

"How are you this evening, my lord?" Lydia said, ignoring Violet and whatever was occurring between her and the duke.

The duke's gaze settled back upon her, and his smile turned genuine rather than taunting. "I am well, Lady Lydia, and better now for seeing you. May I have the honour of the next dance?"

Violet snorted. Lydia raised a brow at her friend, who had merely scowled back at her. "You may," she said, somewhat enjoying her friend's ire. "You may even have the first one."

"Excellent. Shall we?" He held out his arm.

With a smile, she placed her hand on his forearm.

"I'll just wait here, shall I?" Violet said sourly.

Lydia smirked at her friend as the duke led her to the dancing. The first strains of music sounded as they took their places.

She had met the Duke of Meacham the year previous at a ball in Vienna and had struck up a flirtation. It had never moved past an occasional dance and delightful conversation but she had liked him very well. It did not hurt in the slightest that he was beautiful. Overly so, if she were being honest. She much preferred a less god-like man, one who seemed touchable. One with rough edges and long hair and a beard....

"How are you finding the ball, Lady Lydia?" His Grace asked.

Blinking, she brought her thoughts back to the dance. "It is tedious, Your Grace."

He chuckled. "I always did appreciate your directness."

"I am only occasionally direct. Tonight, it appears, is one of those occasions." As they linked hands, she smiled to take the sting from her words.

"I would hope you always felt you could be direct with me, Lady Lydia. I find there is nothing more attractive than a lady who speaks her mind," he said, guiding her to execute the next step.

Arching a brow, she said, "Your Grace, are you telling me what you believe or what you think I want to hear?"

His smile dazzled. "Can it not be both?"

Well, that made her laugh. Still chuckling, she shook her head as they continued the dance.

They spoke of their families, and the time between their last meet and tonight, and compared their journeys from Vienna to London. He was witty and amusing, and before she knew it, the dance was done. Bowing as the final strains sounded, he asked, "May I call on you tomorrow?"

"I would like that."

His smile was warm. "Excellent."

The ballroom had thinned out a little after the last dance, the announcement of refreshments proving an irresistible draw. Delivering her back to her friend, the duke said, "There. Returned to you safely."

Violet sniffed.

That unholy gleam lit his eyes once more. "I should be delighted if you, too, would honour me with a dance, Lady Violet."

"I...can think of no good reason to refuse." The smile she gave was sickly. Taking his arm, she cast a desperate look at Lydia as he led her to the dance floor.

Lydia crossed her eyes in response. Smiling as her friend's scowl was lost in the throng, she idly took up surveying the crowd once more.

"Lady Lydia."

Every muscle in her body tensed. Swallowing, she raised her gaze to meet Oliver's.

Somehow, he had come upon her without her notice. Up close, the impact of him hit her hard. His grey eyes under dark brows. The bold nose almost too big for his face with the bump on the bridge from the time it had been broken. The golden brown hair pulled back from his high forehead and the darker hair on his jaw.

"May I have this dance?" he asked, holding out his arm.

"I—" Damnation, where was her tongue? Staring at his arm, she didn't know what to do. Finally, slowly, she curled her fingers about his forearm. Beneath the cloth of his coat and her gloves, his arm was solid and firm, and she knew it to be corded with muscle. In the privacy of his study, he'd often rolled his shirtsleeves to his elbows and she'd stared at the muscles flexing as he wrote or shuffled paper, at the light sprinkling of dark hair over pale skin, and how she'd wanted to touch and trace.

Her breath caught and she couldn't stop her fingers from digging into the solid flesh.

"Shall—" His voice cracked. Huskily, he continued, "Shall we?"

Wordlessly, she nodded. They arranged themselves amongst the dancers and, when the music started, completed the first steps in silence. Keeping her gaze from him, she concentrated on the moves, the air between them tense and awkward.

"How are you this evening?" he asked.

"I am fine." How much longer could this dance possibly be? It only felt like forever, surely.

"I miss you."

The words startled her so, she stumbled.

He looked chagrined, as if he hadn't meant to speak, but then his lips firmed and he gave a slight nod. "I miss you," he repeated, his tone firm.

Speechless, she stared at him. She had absolutely no idea how to respond.

"I know there is...awkwardness between us, but I should like us to be friends. I miss your friendship, Lydia."

"Do you?" One of the other dancers looked at her, eyebrows raised at the sharpness of her words. With a smile that felt more like a grimace, she ducked her head.

Raising his hand to flank hers, he took the next step. "There has been some unfortunate behaviour, mine as much—if not more so—than yours."

"Unfortunate?" she said, holding on to her smile.

Red stained his cheeks. "I should have handled it better."

She didn't know what to say. This was completely the wrong place to have this conversation. She couldn't yell at him, she couldn't break down, she couldn't admit her love once more. She couldn't do any of these things, and he was looking at her with such caring, such sincerity.

"Lydia."

His voice. His deep, smooth, perfect voice. She couldn't deny him. This had ever been her problem. "Oliver," she said, and in his name was forgiveness and longing and the fact she had missed him, too. She had missed him so much.

He closed his eyes briefly, relief palpable in his expression. It meant this much to him, her friendship. Continuing the steps of the dance, he smiled at her and said something, something about how glad he was they were friends again, and it was all so clear. It was all so horribly, horribly clear.

Her *friendship*.

Something in her broke. She stumbled, the room lurching.

"Lydia?" Concern tinged his expression.

"I am sorry. I am... The heat."

His brow cleared. "Of course. Do you require your mother? I am sure Lady Demartine—"

"No, I need only to return—" Swallowing, she blinked furiously. She hadn't realised she still held out hope, but of course she did. Of *course* she did. How could he not love her? *How*? "Please return me to Violet," she said hoarsely.

"Lydia—"

"Please, Oliver."

Nodding, he led her from the dancing. Violet was nowhere to be seen as they approached a quiet space. Oliver looked around them, but she just wanted him to leave. "Thank you for the dance," she said.

"Should we not wait—"

"Thank you," she interrupted.

Brows drawn, he nodded slowly. "May I call upon you tomorrow?"

"Of course," she said, wrapping her arms about her middle.

He hesitated. "I should not leave you when you are unwell."

"I am fine. It is only the heat. I promise I will be well." She attempted a smile.

He did not look convinced. "Lydia...."

"Perhaps you can bring me a glass of something."

He nodded and, with a purpose, he finally left.

As soon as he disappeared into the crowd, she took a great gasp of air. Oh, it hurt. It hurt so much. Her friendship. Only ever her friendship.

"Lady Lydia, so lovely to see you."

Despair filled her. She closed her eyes, a lump in her throat. Why? Why did this have to happen *now*? Dread pooling within her, she turned. "Lady Seraphina."

Seraphina Waller-Mitchell smiled prettily, her closed fan clasped in her hand. "We did not catch up properly at the Fanning ball. It has been an age since we spoke, surely before you left for the Continent. Remind me again why there was such a rush for you to depart." She raised a thin dark brow, and the insinuation could not have be clearer.

"No reason," Lydia said, wishing herself anywhere but here.

"Ah. Well, it was peculiar and many commented on it at the time. However, that is now past, is it not, and you have such delicious new gossip." Her eyes brightened. "Tell me about the Duke of Meacham. He seems quite taken with you."

She had no idea how to respond and so she didn't.

"Though, if I recall correctly, you had forever set your cap for another." Her smile cut precisely. "Were you not to wed Lord Roxwaithe?"

Lydia had only ever told people close to her about her certainty she would marry Oliver. Her parents knew. Her siblings. Violet. And, when she was young, stupid and under the impression they were friends, she'd told Seraphina Waller-Mitchell. Seraphina Waller-Mitchell was how she had learnt you did not trust everyone.

"Should we expect an announcement shortly?" Seraphina continued. "I have been scouring the papers daily awaiting the bans. Do share what is taking so long."

Holding her elbows, Lydia pressed her arms into her ribs.

Seraphina, of course, did not require a response. "Perhaps it is Lord Roxwaithe has not yet proposed? Whatever could be keeping him? Or is it that he just does not want you."

Holding her chin up, Lydia kept her gaze locked with Seraphina's. She would not let Seraphina Waller-Mitchell see how deeply she cut, she would not.

"Is that it? Did you declare yourself and he refused? He would have done it gently, would he not? Lord Roxwaithe is nothing if not a gentleman."

"Why are you doing this?" she asked, and cursed that her voice cracked.

"Because, my dear." Smiling, she leant forward. "I don't like you."

Lydia could not speak, could only watch as a satisfied smirk settled on the other woman's pink lips.

"Do be sure to invite me to the wedding," Seraphina said, tapping her fan lightly against Lydia's arm. With another smile, she glided into the throng.

Lydia sucked in a breath, but she couldn't get enough air. She couldn't let others see. She couldn't stand here. She couldn't—

She fled.

The room passed in a blur, and the hallway too, and then she found herself in a dark, quiet room. Wrapping her arms about her middle, she sank to the floor. Seraphina was right to mock her. She *was* stupid. She *was* naive. She was so stupidly young, believing a man like Oliver would love her, confusing friendship with love. He had never encouraged her, and every moment, every look she thought to be confirmation she now knew never was, was always nothing more than his friendship.

Taking a shuddering breath, she covered her face with her hands. Friendship. It was what he offered and it was what she would accept. She couldn't not have him in her life. He meant too much...and perhaps everyone was right. It *was* a crush, and she would tell herself that until she believed it.

Chapter Seven

Pulling the bell, Oliver stared impatiently at the door to Torrence House. He'd rushed through that morning's work, had forced himself to eat a sedate lunch and finalise instruction for Rajitha to continue work in the afternoon without him before he'd fairly rushed through his door to hers, taking all of two minutes to clear the space between their houses.

Bouncing on his feet, he fought the urge to bash on the door. What was taking Jonas so long?

Finally, the door swung open, and the butler's dour face cracked a smile. "Lord Roxwaithe. A pleasure, sir."

"As it is to see you, Jonas." He allowed the butler to take his gloves and greatcoat. It was ridiculous to don such for the two minutes it took to get from his house to hers, but society dictated more ridiculous things. "Lady Lydia is at home?"

"She is, my lord. In the blue room. Lady Demartine is with her, and I believe Lord Somerset is also in attendance."

Surprise rose his brows. Harry was here? He hadn't seen Lydia's eldest brother in weeks, Harry obsessed with spending every moment with his betrothed. "Somerset is here?"

The butler's mouth twitched. "I was surprised, too, my lord."

"Well, lead on, Jonas. This I have to see."

Following the butler to the blue room, he pulled at his shirtsleeves as if that would temper the giddy thrum in his veins. The door opened and he found her unerringly, as he always did. She wore a yellow concoction of a dress, a splash of pale sunshine. Her hair was swept up in a complicated arrangement of knots and curls, displaying the smooth column of her neck. The demure fichu hinted at her collarbones and chest and did not quite disguise the swell of her breasts. She laughed, and he found himself smiling, happy he would finally speak with her like they always had. He took a step toward her.

"The Earl of Roxwaithe," Jonas announced hastily.

Red stained his cheeks. In his eagerness, he'd completely ignored protocol. It did not matter, though. Lydia had not heard, instead laughing at something the pup before her—Verdon—said.

The room suddenly took shape. There were people here. So many people, and all of them centred about Lydia. Lady Demartine sat to one side, ostensibly embroidering but clearly enjoying the attention her youngest daughter garnered.

Lydia turned to listen to one of her suitors, the sweep of her neck leading to her barely covered breasts. The fichu was damn near see-through, and he noticed all the men noticing. He wanted to storm through the pack, pull their heads up so their eyes were where they belonged—

Christ. What was he thinking?

Inhaling slowly, he forced himself calm. Lydia was perfectly capable of taking care of herself. He'd observed her do so many, many times, and she'd told him in no uncertain terms she did not require his protection. The last time he'd attempted it, with that cull Whitton, he'd hurt her. No way in hell was he hurting her again.

The boys still clustered around her, competing to draw her attention. Last night when he had suggested this visitation, he had not considered that Lydia was now out. Had not considered others would dance attendance upon her. Had not considered the season had yet one more week, and both she, her brothers and her sister would have friends and admirers visit their home. He'd, stupidly, thought he would have her to himself.

"It's a bit like Bedlam, isn't it?" Beside him, Harry Torrence regarded his sister with a bewildered kind of pride. "I don't know how she gets them to come to heel," the young Lord Somerset continued. "She's like the Pied Piper, but with men of aristocracy."

"Is it always like this?" Oliver asked, hoping like hell he'd disguised the fact he hadn't noticed Harry's presence until he'd spoken.

"More often than not. Lydia is a bit of a hit, you know."

Harry Torrence, the master of understatement.

"I believe Father refuses suits for her hand—*suits*, you understand—almost daily."

Oliver's head whipped around. Too fast. "What?"

Rolling his eyes, Harry amended, "Maybe not that often, but it might as well be. She's made quite the impression. It's a bit disconcerting, really. *I* remember frog spawn in my slippers. Gave me a deathly fear of nightwear." He shuddered.

Oliver rubbed the crick in his neck. The throng around Lydia had thinned a little, but there was still a gaggle of young men vying for her attention. Harry was right. It *was* Bedlam.

"What brings you here, Roxwaithe?" Harry asked. "It's been an age since you attended one of these events."

"Thought I'd visit with the family. It has, as you say, been a while."

"You'll stay for dinner, won't you? Another hour, and these people will be gone. Tessa's coming with her parents this evening, and you haven't met her properly yet." Harry fairly glowed at the mention of his betrothed.

"Of course. It would be a delight to dine with your family and your fiancée." What would it be like to feel so strongly about another person, it burst from you? His gaze slid to Lydia. She was holding court admirably, making sure each buck was heard but none favoured.

Lydia's gaze found him. A glorious smile lit her face, genuine and blinding. A thrum began in his veins, and he took half a step toward her.

"Lydia's got you on her hook, too."

"Pardon?" He dragged his gaze back.

Shaking his head, Harry regarded him with a grin. "Damn, Alexandra was right. I owe her a guinea."

Brow creasing, he said, "I don't understand."

"No, but you will." Harry's gaze slid to his sister. "She always did say."

"Say what?" But Harry had already left.

Frowning, Oliver regarded Lydia. What was that all about? She found his gaze again and, the barest hint of a smile playing about her lips, she surreptitiously rolled her eyes. He raised a brow in response, Harry's odd comments forgotten.

It took only a moment to be by her side. "Lady Lydia." He tried not to smirk at the radiance of her smile, brighter than any he'd seen her give another.

"Oliv— Roxwaithe. You have come." She beamed up at him and her warmth invaded him, making his heart light and he wanted to grin in return but first....

He looked at the lad opposite her. The lad blanched and abandoned his seat. Oliver replaced him. The others clustered about her watched him warily and, one by one, they offered their apologies to Lydia and departed. Well, all but one.

"Tell us, Roxwaithe, why do you come?" Verdon blustered.

"Why should I not?" he said, his tone chilled.

Verdon blanched. "I had not thought to see you here, is all," he stammered.

Stretching his arm along the back of the settee, Oliver levelled a stare on him.

Lord Verdon shot to his feet. "I beg your pardon, Lady Lydia, I did not notice the time. I must be on my way."

"Of course." She waited until Verdon had cleared the door before raising a brow at Oliver. "You do know how to scatter a room."

He shrugged. "It is a gift. Do you like any of them?"

"I like all of them," she said, picking up her needlework.

"Any one in particular?"

"Don't try that with me. It won't work."

"What won't work?"

"That. That look. Your *I am the Earl of Roxwaithe* look."

"I don't have a look," he said, giving her the earl look.

"No, of course not. You, however, shouldn't be such a bully," she said mildly.

"I am not a bully. I said nothing. The lads could have stayed."

"Yes, because the Earl of Roxwaithe deploying his censure is a lightweight thing of no consequence."

With a shrug, he concealed his smirk. He'd missed this. "You seem to be quite popular."

"I am most fortunate to be visited by such fine gentlemen."

He snorted.

"What?"

"You say that with a straight face."

"Of course. They are fine men of my age. Why would I not?"

"They seem so—" Young. He was going to say young, but Lydia was young also. He shook himself. "Nothing. Apologies for running them off. Shall I fetch them back?"

"No. I would rather talk with you, now we are friends again."

Their eyes locked. She wet her lips, slightly reddened by her teeth. She always worried her bottom lip when she concentrated, white teeth biting into plump flesh, and her breasts rose and fell beneath the sorry excuse for a fichu. She'd changed in the year and a half she'd been away. There was more polish to her and she did seem...older, for want of a better word.

The air grew heavy, and his fingers itched to trace her hairline, push the tendrils back, follow a line down her cheek, her neck. He'd cover her chest with his hand, feel the rapid rise and fall, count her breaths, his smallest finger less than an inch from the swell of her breasts.

"His Grace, the Duke of Meacham."

Jonas's words rang throughout the room.

Breaking their gaze, Oliver straightened guiltily as Meacham made his way toward Lydia. "I apologise to be visiting so late in the day, my lady," he said, bowing low over her hand.

"It is no issue, Your Grace." Expression clearing, she offered a smile. "May I present the Earl of Roxwaithe?"

"We have met." Meacham cast an assessing eye over Oliver.

Stone-faced, he returned the duke's perusal.

The corner of Meacham's lip lifted, though his eyes hardened.

Lydia looked between them and sighed. "Really?" she said, almost to herself.

Keeping his gaze on Meacham, he said, "You are recently returned to London, are you not, Meacham?"

"I am. I had the acquaintance of Lady Lydia in Vienna and am eager to renew it." Sitting on the divan, he arranged himself carelessly and, though he smiled, there was an edge behind it.

Inwardly, Oliver scowled. The man was too good-looking for his own good.

"Roxwaithe." Lady Demartine called from the other side of the room. "Please, come help me."

Without thought, he stood and strode to her. "What is amiss, my lady?"

"I seem to have misplaced my yellow skein. Help me find it?"

"Of course." He glanced over at Lydia and Meacham. She was laughing at something Meacham had said, her expression bright. Oliver scowled.

"Ah, here it is," Lady Demartine said, producing a ball of yellow thread. "I must have been sitting on it."

He glanced again at Lydia and Meacham. "If you no longer require my assistance—"

"I believe Demartine was asking for you, Roxwaithe," she said calmly. "Something about drainage in Yorkshire?"

"He was?"

"Yes. You should go seek him out. It seemed quite urgent."

"Drainage?"

"Yes." Lady Demartine did not lose her smile. "I'm sure Lydia and His Grace will not mind. They are in the midst of becoming better acquainted, and you do not wish to interfere with that, do you Roxwaithe?"

He swallowed. "No, my lady."

"Good. Find Demartine, Roxwaithe. Discuss drainage." Her smile sweetened. "Now."

"Yes, my lady." He gave one last glance at Lydia. She was wholly absorbed in whatever tale Meacham imparted and had not noticed his absence.

Rubbing his chest, he left the sitting room. Lord Demartine was in his study, and he looked up in surprise when Oliver entered. "Roxwaithe? What are you doing here?"

He hovered at the threshold. "Lady Demartine said—"

"She did?" His gaze turned shrewd. "Lydia is entertaining guests, isn't she?"

"She is."

"Of course she is." He shook his head ruefully. "Well, don't just stand there, Roxwaithe. Come in."

Closing the door behind him, he sat in his usual spot opposite Lord Demartine. Guilt crept over him. Lydia was this man's daughter. The man who treated him almost as a son, who had guided him through those first hellish years of being Roxwaithe. If he knew....

He ran a hand over his beard. He needed these thoughts under control. She was an attractive young woman. Surely any man would occasionally feel as he did. It meant nothing. He would simply push such thoughts to a corner of his mind labelled "Lydia" and resolve not to think such again.

"Here to see Lydia, were you?"

Oliver glanced up. Rubbing his lip, Lord Demartine regarded him. "I beg your pardon, sir?"

"It's been a while since you've visited Torrence House. Lady Demartine tells me you and Lydia danced at the ball last night. Seems every man under the age of fifty has decided to descend upon my door." Lord Demartine shook his head. "We didn't have this problem with Alexandra. A normal number of suitors for her, though she's yet to choose one."

Oliver stared at the paper before him. It took all his control not to react.

Lord Demartine leaned back. "You know Meacham, don't you, Roxwaithe?"

"Yes, sir."

"I believe Lydia got to know him in Vienna. Lady Demartine quite likes him. Worthy young man, don't you think?"

"Yes, sir."

"Lydia could do worse. Has a few seasons under his belt, though. Nine years is not too big a difference between husband and wife. I should like Lydia to marry someone she cares for."

"Yes, sir."

"It will more than likely happen this season. One shouldn't wait, if one *were* waiting."

He didn't respond,

Lord Demartine sighed. "I tried," he said, almost to himself. "You are staying for dinner, yes? We dine *en familie* tonight, sans Alexandra. She's disappeared to Bentley Close, probably to investigate those reports of ghostly activity. She always believed herself stealthy, but I know my children." He stood. "My stomach is telling me it is close to the dinner hour. Let us head to the dining room. I'm sure there'll be something to tide us over until the first course."

Oliver followed Lord Demartine from the study, the dining room only a short walk. Lady Demartine had already arrived and Lord Demartine headed straight for his wife, brushing the top of her head with his lips before seating himself. Oliver trailed him...and stopped stock still when he saw the Duke of Meacham seated beside Lydia.

"Come sit by me, Roxwaithe. It has been an age since we caught up," Lady Demartine said warmly.

He seated himself, and spent the rest of the evening resisting the urge to glare as Lydia and Meacham flirted their way through the meal.

Chapter Eight

THE THEATRE STALLS WERE quickly filling. Arms folded on the theatre box's balcony edge, Lydia watched as those dressed in their finery took their seats. One lady wore the most exquisite worsted silk gown in a strikingly bold shade of orange. Not many women would be able to pull off such a colour, but the lady's dark skin and darker hair perfectly complemented the sunset tone. Lydia was envious. Lord knew the shade would look horrible on her.

"Ah, this is delightful. Sitting here, waiting for the play to commence, and being completely ignored by my companion. Exactly what I had hoped for this evening."

She glanced over her shoulder. Oliver lounged in his seat, a playbill held loose in his hand and the most overly exaggerated mournful look on his face she had ever seen.

Ignoring his dramatics, she plucked the playbill from him. "What are we watching?"

Oliver stared at his now empty hand. "Did you just snatch that?"

Ignoring him again, she perused the programme. "Oh. Shakespeare."

"You did. You snatched it. From my hand."

"Honestly, you would think nobody in the theatre community at large had an ounce of creativity or originality. And they call it the creative arts."

"From. My. Hand."

She levelled him a stare. "Are you going to be tiresome about this?"

"Maybe."

"Fine." She shoved the playbill at him.

"And now you shove things at me. What did I do to deserve this treatment?"

"You invited me and my parents to the Roxwaithe theatre box. You have no one to blame but yourself."

"'Tis true. It is my tragedy. And even worse Lord and Lady Demartine were subsequently invited to the Duke of Marylebone's box, abandoning me to your tender mercies."

"Woe is you."

He nodded gravely. "Woe is indeed me."

Mirth bubbling over, she grinned. Tapping the playbill against his leg, he grinned in return as he leant back in his chair. The fabric of his breeches stretched over his thighs, outlining powerful muscles. Unable to help herself, she stared, her mouth drying as she traced the length of his thigh, the turn of his hip, the narrow waist concealed by his appropriately sombre waistcoat. The hair gathered behind his neck revealed the strong lines of his face. His nose was bold, perhaps a little too much, but it perfectly balanced his strong jaw accentuated by his beard. His full lips—kissing lips, she'd always thought—were pursed thoughtfully, and she'd like nothing so much as to soothe his furrowed brow and then run her fingers over those kissing lips to ascertain for herself if they were was soft as she remembered....

Damnation.

Tearing her gaze from him, she closed her eyes. She had promised herself she wouldn't look at him so. She had promised herself she would treat him as she would Harry or George or Michael, but he was not her brother, and she'd never been able to look from him.

Oliver exhaled heavily.

Opening her eyes, she regarded his left ear. "What is it?"

He shrugged.

"Oliver. You have your concerned look. What are you concerned about?"

"Stephen," he finally said. "He has decided he wishes to join Alexandra in studying the spiritual."

Shock stole her tongue. "What?"

"I know." He rubbed his neck.

"But he's never shown an interest."

"I know."

"*Never*, Oliver."

"Believe me, I know."

"Why would he say such a thing?"

"I don't know. Why does Stephen do anything?"

Her mind raced. "There must be a reason. Stephen is always purposeful."

"No, he's not."

Oh, good Lord. "Oliver," she said pleasantly. "You are an idiot."

His eyebrows shot up. "No one speaks to me as you do."

"That's because you've somehow convinced everyone you are fearsome."

"I *am* fearsome."

She snorted.

"Fine. How am I being idiotic?"

"You wear blinders where your brother is concerned, and you do not regard him with the same lens as the rest of us. To you, he is your little brother, your *remaining* brother, and you view him as if he were still a child. You are aware he is almost thirty-one?"

A scowl settled on his features. "I am well aware of my brother's age."

"Good. Because you act as if you are not."

"No, I don't."

"Oliver, he is allowed to be aimless."

His jaw tensed.

She sighed. "Oliver, your path was set for you from the moment of your birth. You always knew what lay ahead and what responsibilities it would hold. For the rest of us, it is confusing, and even a little terrifying, to consider what life might hold for us."

Eyes downcast, he said, "Do you feel this way?"

"Sometimes. I am supposed to marry, and marry well. I always thought—" Her cheeks heated. She really didn't need to remind him she'd always thought she'd marry *him*. "I know the path of my life, but it is now changed and I am not certain precisely where it will lead. That can be daunting. Alexandra has gone to Bentley Close," she said, changing the subject suddenly. "Do you think Stephen has gone with her?"

"No, he is still in London—You're funning me, aren't you?" he asked resignedly.

"Maybe just a little."

He shook his head ruefully. "Alexandra has gone to Bentley Close? I suppose she will end up at Waithe Hall."

"Most likely. She is determined, you know."

"I know."

"She left a day ago. Mama and Papa believe her to be visiting relatives." She gave him a stern look. "You are not to tell them differently."

"I won't."

Surprise filled her. "Really?"

"You have asked me not to."

"I thought you told my father everything. I thought it was almost a religion with you."

His lips twisted, but he didn't deny it. "You should know, though, your father is not fooled. He believes she is at Bentley Close, investigating ghosts and such."

She exhaled. "I knew it was doomed to failure."

"She came to see me," he continued. "She wanted to know about reports of lights at Waithe."

"Lights?"

"The villagers reported lights in the windows of the east wing late at night, no doubt the work of spirits. There was that housekeeper, the one who searched for the lost keys. Maxim and your sister always used to—" His smile faded as an old pain shadowed his eyes. "It hits me at odd times, and never when I expect." He looked at her. "Do you remember him?"

Wishing she could heal his hurt, she reached out, placing her hand on his forearm. "Yes, but I never knew him well. He was always Alexandra's."

He exhaled. "I know. It was impossible to separate them. Your mother used to try, but it was always doomed to failure. They would inevitably find their way back to each other." The corner of his lip lifted.

What memory did he see to cause that small smile? "I wish he were here, Oliver. I wish you, Stephen and Maxim were with one another, and you were just as annoyed with Maxim's choices as you are with Stephen's."

His smile grew. "Back on that, are we?"

"We were never going to not discuss it," she said archly. He'd needed distraction, and she was more than willing to provide it.

"What, then, is the solution?"

"There is no solution."

He blinked. "Pardon?"

"Stephen is a man grown. You really ought to treat him as such. You cannot fix this for him. It is something that is his to discover."

"But—"

"Oliver. You cannot fix this for him."

Exhaling, he nodded, his gaze drifting to her hand. Of a sudden, she realised she'd never let him go. There was an intimacy to their pose, one she had no claim to, but one she'd always desperately wanted.

His eyes met hers, dark and unreadable. Breath locked in her chest, she wanted nothing more than to move closer to him, to feel those strong arms around her, to feel the hardness of his chest beneath her fingers as she leaned forward and brushed his lips with hers, once, twice, before he cracked and kissed her, truly kissed her, licking at her lips, his tongue invading her, his hands tightening on her back as he drew her closer....

"Lady Lydia."

Cheeks aflame, she jerked back. The Duke of Meacham stood at the door to the Roxwaithe box, his gaze shifting between her and Oliver. Quickly she stood, dipping into a curtsey while Oliver also rose, more slowly, his bow considerably more forced.

Arranging a smile on her face, Lydia rose from her curtsey. "Your Grace."

"Lady Lydia. Your father gave me direction to you. I did not expect to find you alone...with Lord Roxwaithe." His gaze again shifted between them.

"It is my box," Oliver said.

"Yes, of course," His Grace said smoothly. "Lady Lydia, would you grant me the honour of escorting you to the refreshments at intermission? I hoped to continue our discussion on aqueducts in antiquity."

"Do you have something of particular to discuss?" she asked.

"I discovered a book my dealer tells me is quite rare, and I should like to gain your opinion on both it and its contents."

Her lips quirked. The duke had discovered her interest quickly and sought to take advantage. How enterprising of him. "I should like that very much, Your Grace."

"Lady Lydia, you know you have leave to refer me by name."

Beside her, Oliver stiffened.

"Yes. Thank you. Meacham." She resisted the urge to glance at Oliver.

"I'm sure the earl won't mind losing your company for a time. Will you, Roxwaithe?" Meacham's smile took on an edge.

Eyes hard, Oliver worked his jaw. What he had to be annoyed about, she had no idea. "Of course not," he said.

"Excellent. I shall return at intermission." Meacham bent low over her hand, his lips the barest whisper through the fine leather of her glove. "Until then, my lady," he murmured and, with a final smile, he exited the box.

After Lord Meacham left, Lydia arranged her skirts, fiddled with her gloves, and generally did not look at Oliver. Her neck felt hot, as did her cheeks, and a strange churn had begun in her belly. Good Lord, this was ridiculous. She had no reason to feel guilty. Oliver was merely her friend. He did not want her. He had made that quite, quite clear. She had a right to flirt with other men, to meet them at intermission and talk of shared interests, and if she chose to find a secluded corner with Meacham, Oliver had no cause to complain. She had no reason to feel guilty.

Taking a breath, she said brightly, "How do you think this production will butcher Shakespeare?"

Oliver remained silent, his hard gaze trained straight ahead.

"Maybe it will surprise us and, I don't know, actually be intriguing? After all, most of society is here. Surely they will attempt something that approaches entertainment."

A muscle ticked in his jaw.

"Although horrendous can be entertainment in itself." Still no response. "Oliver, what is wrong?"

"Nothing," he ground out.

"If it is nothing, why won't you talk with me?"

"I do not feel like conversing."

"That is peculiar, seeing not ten minutes ago, you very much felt like conversing. Why do you not now?"

"Because, Lydia."

"That is not a reason."

He shrugged.

The silence between them filled with tension. She folded the fabric of her dress through her fingers, working her jaw as a vast wave of nothing emanated from him.

Finally, she'd had enough. "I am going to sit with my parents. Give the duke my direction at intermission."

"Don't you mean Meacham?" he said snidely.

Giving him a hard glare, she swept from the box. Her annoyance remained with her as she settled herself in Marylebone's box with her parents. She hoped Oliver enjoyed watching the play by himself. She hoped he had all manner of fun seated alone in his box, watching as this troupe mangled Shakespeare horribly. And when Meacham came to escort her to the refreshments, she was going to laugh and be merry and not give a damn what Oliver Farlisle, the Earl of Roxwaithe, had to say about it.

Chapter Nine

Lydia attacked the easel, her brow creased as she stabbed with her brush. From where he stood, Oliver couldn't see much of what she was painting, but it looked like an array of variously shaped green blobs with the occasional brown blob thrown in for contrast. If one squinted, one could concede her painting vaguely resembled the plants surrounding them in the conservatory. If one squinted.

He watched her in silence for a moment, not wanting to destroy her version of tranquillity. She always painted when she wanted calm, and the fact she was terrible at it did not deter her at all. Tendrils of red-gold hair lay against her neck and curled softly against her shoulders, the rest of it gathered into some complicated braided thing at the crown of her head. The back of her gown dipped between her shoulder blades, a soft vee displaying warm, creamy skin. Her blades moved as she stabbed at the easel and he charted their progress, wondering how the skin would feel beneath a splayed hand as she reached for a kiss rather than a paintbrush—

Shaking himself, he scowled at his distraction. He was here to apologise, not to ogle her without her knowledge. "Are you destroying another sheet of paper?"

She whirled around, her brows drawing as she spied him. For the longest time, they stared at each other.

"You're dripping paint," he finally said.

She skewered the paintbrush into a water-filled jar. "What are you doing here, Oliver?"

"I came to see Lord Demartine." Her expression didn't change. "And to apologise."

Her expression softened. Slightly. "Oh?"

"Yes." Feeling awkward, he rubbed the back of his neck. "I apologise for my behaviour at the theatre. I was boorish."

"You were." She studied him a moment. With a sigh, she shook her head. "However, I am creating a masterpiece. You should not disturb genius." The corner of her lips tilted.

Relief flowed through him. She forgave him. Taking a place behind her, he studied the composition. "Genius?"

"It is not my fault you don't recognise artistry when it is before you." Glancing over her shoulder, she arched a brow.

He always forgot how beautiful she was. He knew it on some base level, but to him she was Lydia, her face and form merely one part of her. She had been declared a diamond of the first order, and men fell over themselves to be the one to put a smile on her face, but it was more than her face. It was her. Her wit, her joy, the way she teased. The way she teased *him*. The counsel she gave. The fact she adored architecture and left hair pins littered everywhere, and when she was with him, he felt...complete.

"Did you really come to see my father?" she asked.

"No," he admitted.

She beamed, and he smiled in return, helpless not to. "So you merely came to critique genius artwork?"

"This? This is genius?"

"It is the genesis of genius."

"Of course." He studied the easel, debating if he should ask about Meacham. He had just apologised, she had accepted, but he didn't know how solid the foundation of their relationship. Before, he would have asked without thought, but that was before. *Just ask, man.* "You have been spending time with the Duke of Meacham," he blurted.

She regarded her painting as well. "Yes," she said. "He is courting me."

"Good. That is good. He is..." He trailed off, uncertain how to continue. What to say? In the end, he said nothing.

She glanced at him. "I should like your opinion. He is courting me, Oliver, with serious intent. I believe he has spoken to Papa." Her gaze turned imploring. "I need your opinion on the rest of my life."

Just barely, he held on to his neutral expression. He didn't want to talk with her about this. He didn't want to know she would eventually be someone's fiancée, someone's wife, however, he had no choice. He had declared himself her friend. He *was* her friend. He would help her with this. Because they were friends. "Do you like him?"

She stared at the painting. "I think I *could* like him," she finally said.

"But you don't know?" He shouldn't feel pleasure at the thought.

"I don't know him well enough to *know*, though it doesn't really matter." Her expression turned bleak. "If not him, it will be someone else, someone I'll dance with once or twice, see at a few events, and then he will ask my father for permission to propose. And I should say yes, because it is the right thing to do. For my family. For me. The thing is, though, I don't know if I will *know* him. What if we do not suit? What if we marry, and then five years after we dislike each other, and we live in the same house but have separate lives? I don't want to have a separate life from my husband, Oliver. I don't want to hear about mistresses and opera singers and.... I want to have what Mama and Papa have. I want a person I know so well I can always trust him." Hazel eyes caught his. "Am I naïve?"

"No, Lydia." His hand twitched. He wanted to cup her face, swipe his thumb over her cheek, rid her of uncertainty and worry. "Of course not."

She wrapped her arms about herself. "I have never had to think about this before."

"Why?" he asked.

She looked at him sharply.

Christ. Stupid, idiotic, *thoughtless* comment. Because she had always thought to marry *him*.

"What about you?" she asked quickly. "Do you like anyone? You have not courted anyone seriously since.... Was it Elizabeth Grainger?"

He stared at her blankly.

"Lord Palmeroy's daughter?" she prompted.

"I did not court her."

"*I* remember quite clearly you courting her. Everyone thought you did."

"Well, everyone was wrong." He barely remembered Elizabeth Grainger. He was fairly sure he'd seen her at a few events, had perhaps even danced with her, and from this society had decided he had been courting her? "I have not given serious thought to anyone."

"But you have given an unserious thought?"

He didn't respond.

Her smile died. "Really? Who?"

"It is a thought, nothing more."

"Who?"

"No one in particular, however, 'the Roxwaithe name must carry on'."

She cocked her head. "Is that your father you are quoting?"

"Who else?"

"He is dead, Oliver."

"And yet I still hear his voice in my head." He exhaled. "Do not listen to me, I am being maudlin. We should instead focus on this travesty on the easel."

"It is not a travesty; it is a work of staggering genius."

"Of course it is." Turning, she grinned at him and he saw the streak of paint on her jaw. Without thought, he raised his hand to wipe it clean.

Her startled gaze flew to his. Fingers cupping her neck, his thumb rested on her jaw. Mesmerised, he watched her lips part, as she wet the soft flesh. This was how a suitor would stand before her. He would want to trace the line of her jaw, feather his thumb over her full lower lip. He would want to see her eyes darken and her chest rise, watch the drift of her gaze to his own lips. He would curl his hand around the back of her neck, his fingers spearing into her hair, as he drew her to him, as he lowered his head, as he covered her mouth with his. He would want desperately to touch her, to discover if the skin of her chest was as soft as it looked. He would want to determine the exact weight of her breast, and the sound she would make when he toyed with her nipple. He would do all those things, and more. Her suitor.

Jerking his hand from her, he said hoarsely, "You had paint."

She blinked.

"On your cheek." He cleared his throat. "You must have wiped your cheek. It's gone now."

"Oh." Great hazel eyes glanced to the side. Then back at him. She shook her head. "Paint. Yes. I—"

"The Duke of Meacham is here to see you."

They both looked to the door. Jonas stood just inside the conservatory, his face impassive.

Lydia's eyes cleared. "Of course, Jonas. Thank you. Please tell His Grace I will be with him shortly."

"Yes, my lady." He bowed and departed.

"I shall leave you to your guest," Oliver said.

"Oliver, you should not—"

He forced a smile. "No, see to your guest. We will visit tomorrow. Or are you to the park?"

"Probably to the park, but Oliver—"

"Tomorrow," he said, and left the conservatory.

As he entered Roxegate, he told himself he hadn't run from her. She had a visitor. It was right and correct he left so she could attend to him. Even if it was Meacham.

A sour feeling settled in his stomach.

It was none of his concern if Meacham chose to court her. None of his concern, bar she was happy. He wanted her always to be happy.

Perhaps he should seek a wife. Maybe a sensible widow, or an aging wallflower. Or perhaps he wouldn't marry at all. Perhaps Stephen could carry the mantle, and perhaps his brother would finally find purpose in the role of father and sire of the Foxwaithe heir. Although he, Oliver, should like children, their bright hazel eyes looking up at him as they shouted a greeting, and their mother tickling them and chasing them, her hair a red-gold stream behind her—

Exhaling, he tugged at the knot of hair at his nape. He wanted Lydia to be happy, and if Meacham made her happy, then he would smile, he would congratulate them at their wedding, and he would bounce their children on his knee. He wanted, above all things, for her to be happy, and if he, on the other hand, wasn't....

He rubbed his hand over his face. By God, he would be happy *for* her. Even if it killed him.

Chapter Ten

THE LATE AFTERNOON SUN made long shadows of the trees and more people wore heavy attire than not, but that hadn't stopped most of London turning out to promenade around Hyde Park.

It also hadn't stopped Violet from insisting on breaking in her new phaeton. The phaeton lurched forward and, bracing herself, Lydia gripped the side, her fingers digging into the soft lining. Unfortunately, Violet was not the most talented driver.

Laughing nervously, Violet gathered the reins in her hands. "I promise you, I have this under control."

"Of course." Lydia removed her claw-like grip from the padded edge.

"Simon showed me only yesterday the best way to steer the horses."

"Steer?"

"Drive. Whatever."

"I don't think your brother is the most reliable source of information. Did he not crash his phaeton last week?"

"That was on Rotten Row. He was going entirely too fast. I shall not do the same." Violet urged the horses forward and they, seemingly confused, somehow still managed to take a step in the general direction they were headed.

Turning her head, Lydia ignored the stop-start of the phaeton as they slowly picked their way along Ladies' Mile. As long as she didn't observe Violet's attempt to drive the phaeton, all would be well. That was how it worked, surely.

Tugging on the reins, Violet struggled to contain the horses, who seemed to be interested in anything but pulling the phaeton. "I don't understand." Brows drawn, Violet stared at the horses. "Even *Anne* is competent at this."

"Your sister has been horse-mad since she was in leading strings. Remind me, when did you learn to drive a pair? Yesterday," Lydia answered her own question. "It was yesterday."

Violet shot her an annoyed look, only to have the most ferocious scowl overtake on her features. "Dear God."

"What is it?" Turning, she followed Violet's line of sight. There really was only one person who inspired such loathing in her friend, and she smiled when she saw him. "Ah. The Duke of Meacham approaches."

Her friend's scowl grew more thunderous. "Why is *he* coming over?"

"Because he is a polite gentleman who has the acquaintance of us both?"

"Would that he forgot our connection," Violet muttered.

Lydia tutted. "You won't attract a husband with that attitude."

Her friend snorted.

Meacham approached, smile wide as he placed a boot on the phaeton's step. "Lady Lydia, how fortunate. I was hoping I might see you."

"And I, you, Your Grace. You remember Lady Violet Crafers?"

"I do." His grin turned to a smirk. "Lady Violet, you cut quite a swathe through the carriages of Ladies' Mile. Truly, I have never seen such...enthusiasm at the reins in my life."

Violet glared at him, and quite pointedly offered no greeting.

As surreptitiously as she could, Lydia elbowed her.

"Hello, Your Grace," Violet said reluctantly.

His smile widened. Turning his gaze to Lydia, he said, "Lady Lydia, would you care to walk with me?"

Violet opened her mouth.

"I'll have her back to you safe and sound, Lady Violet," he said, cutting her off.

Sulkily, Violet crossed her arms.

"I cannot walk with you, sir. I wear not the correct footwear." Lydia brandished her feet.

He glanced at the sturdy leather books she wore. "So I see, my lady," he said gravely. "Such delicate articles should not make contact with the ground. I shall shuck my coat and your feet need never touch the rude earth."

"I could never allow you to do such a thing. Your jacket is too exquisite. Your cloak, however...."

"Yes. My cloak is a sad item of clothing. It would do well as a sacrifice for a lady."

They grinned at each other.

"You two are so peculiar," Violet said sourly.

The duke smirked. Holding out his arm, he said to Lydia, "Shall we?"

Grinning in return, she took his arm and descended from the phaeton. "Let's."

They strolled along the Mile. "How is your family?" Meacham asked.

"They are well. My father asks your opinion on the current bond market. I believe you were speaking of it previously?"

"Yes, we were. I shall be sure to send him a note." He glanced at her. "Your sister was to travel, was she not?"

"She was. To our family estate in Northumberland."

"I have long admired Lady Alexandra. She follows her own path."

What an exquisite way to say her sister was odd. "She does indeed. You know of her interest?"

"I do. It is intriguing, and she writes eloquently of it."

"You have read her articles?"

"I have. She is much taken with Waithe Hall. The story of the housekeeper with the lost keys is a particular favourite."

"Good Lord, I have heard that story over and over. She is forever discussing it. Oliver says—That is, Lord Roxwaithe is amused by her interest, and as our families are close, he is happy for her to investigate the tale and its origin."

He was silent a moment. "You are often with Lord Roxwaithe."

"I am. I grew up with him, and he and my father often discuss business. He is as a brother to me." The claim felt like ash on her tongue. She had not, nor had she ever, regarded Oliver as a brother, however, perhaps if she said the words enough, she would believe them.

"A brother." He was silent a moment. "And Lord George still tours the Continent?"

"He does." She glanced at him. His gaze was forward, his expression considering. "My parents seek to join him in the coming month."

"And will you, as well?"

"I had not considered it, but perhaps."

"If I may say, I would hope you remain in London. There would be many who would miss you, should you decide to leave England's shores."

She didn't know how to reply. She knew Meacham sought to court her, but this was as blatant as he'd ever been.

"Although I would warrant your interest in architecture was piqued by your own journey to the Continent."

She'd mentioned her interest once, in passing, during a dance. Impressive that he'd twice now remembered. "I am happy with the architecture of London. There is much to discover, if one but looks."

"Indeed there is. Speaking of which, there is a lecture on the repair and reconstruction of St Paul's on Thursday next. I believe there may even be a viewing of Wren's original notes. It would delight me if you would allow me to escort you."

She tilted her head. He had clearly done his research, and was determined in his suit. She did like him. She had enjoyed their time together in Vienna, and this time in London. She could entertain his suit. Perhaps he would be someone she could picture her life with. "I should like that very much."

His eyes lit with warmth before glancing past her. "I should return you to Lady Violet before her scowls set me to flame."

She looked at her friend. Sure enough, Violet shot them looks that clearly spoke of his demise.

A devil took her. "Perhaps we should walk further. I feel the need for exercise."

"But your friend—"

"Yes. My friend." She raised her brow.

A slow smile dawned on his features. "Indeed, Lady Lydia. Perhaps we shall take the long way?"

"Perhaps we shall." Linking arms with him, they made sure they strolled. For a long time.

***

AT PACE, OLIVER STRODE down Ladies' Mile. If he'd had any goddamn sense, he would have a horse made available for this jaunt to Hyde Park but apparently his brain was not working as it should. Instead, he'd rushed from Roxegate as if the fires of hell pursued him, and without any thought. He was lucky he'd remembered a hat, coat, gloves and walking stick, and even then it was because his butler had pressed them upon him.

Quickening his pace, he scanned those who paraded looking for Lydia. He'd tried to work all afternoon, but his mind kept wandering, and then he would think of something and want to tell Lydia. Finally, he'd given in. She'd said she was going for a drive with her friend Violet in Hyde Park, so here he was, weaving in and out of societal traffic.

"Roxwaithe!"

Brows drawn, he turned. Wainwright approached, a stupid grin on his handsome face.

"What are you doing here?" Oliver asked. "Shouldn't you be in the country?"

"Lady Wainwright decided we must remain in London until the season officially ended and I am, as always, her slave. Besides which, there was a cracking football match between Westminster and Eton on Saturday that I thought I should attend. For reasons."

"Of course."

"What are you doing here? Can't remember the last time I saw you in Hyde Park." He looked Oliver up and down. "And on foot."

"No reason."

"Well, don't look now, but your 'no reason' is walking with a duke."

He almost wrenched his neck turning so fast. Lydia did indeed walk with Meacham, their heads close. She laughed, her hand swatting the man's forearm.

Anger, annoyance tore through him. He refused to label it jealousy.

Wainwright shook his head. "Yes, I can see that nothing at all has tempted you from your study."

"It *is* nothing. I merely thought to tell her of a lecture I saw advertised. She has an interest in architecture."

"Yes, I know. You have told me. Many, many times." Wainwright looked at him curiously. "You are aware men our age marry women her age all the time."

"What?"

"Take her duke. He is only four years our younger."

"Five."

"Four. Five. He is still almost a decade older than her."

"But she is not marrying him."

"Yet. She is not marrying him *yet*."

A protest leapt, but he wrestled it silent.

"Someone will marry her, you know," Wainwright said. "Why can't it be you?"

Oliver stabbed at the ground with his walking stick. "I don't feel that way."

Wainwright started to laugh, only to cut off abruptly when Oliver didn't join him. "Oh. You are serious."

"She deserves someone her own age."

"Doesn't she deserve the person she wants? And, from all accounts, that person is you."

"She wants Meacham."

"Well. You would know."

"Why did you say it like that?"

"Like what?"

"Snidely."

Of course Wainwright didn't answer. Bloody bastard. "I saw your brother the other night," his friend said instead. "He was with the Waller-Mitchell girl."

"Who?" Waller-Mitchell…. Was she the woman who always gave Lydia grief? "Why was he with her?"

"I don't know. It was only for a moment, but you don't want to allow that relationship to continue. The girl is trouble."

"I know. I'll speak to him." He glanced at Lydia. She was still with Meacham. Brows drawing, he watched them. They made a handsome couple. His gaze wandered over her. She was so pretty. So full of wit and intelligence. Why wouldn't Meacham want her? Why wouldn't any man?

Wainwright watched him closely. "Yes. You clearly have no feelings for her."

"Do you have any plans?" he asked his friend abruptly.

"I have the strangest feeling I am about to."

"Come to the club. Let us see the newest whiskies they have available."

"I shall come, but know Lady Wainwright expects me home for our evening meal."

"We will have you home well before then." Turning on his heel, he did the right thing.

He let Lydia go.

Chapter Eleven

Unlacing the ribbon beneath her chin, Lydia removed her bonnet. "It's been a day, Jonas," she said to the Torrence butler. "There was absolutely nothing of interest in the shops, and there was hardly any good gossip besides. Did you know Roger Crittinden is attempting to cross the channel in a rowboat?"

"I had heard, my lady," Jonas said gravely, taking her proffered bonnet. "I believe it is a wager with Lord Lilwhythe."

"Both of them, less than half a brain between them." She shrugged off her pelisse.

"The Duke of Meacham has been awaiting your arrival, my lady."

She paused in removing her gloves. She had not been aware Meacham was to visit today. "How long has he been waiting?"

"Not long, my lady. I believe Lord Harry entertained him for a brief while before he was called away."

Well, that was horrifying. Harry would, and frequently did, talk the ear off anyone who would listen, and always on the most inappropriate topics. It was vastly fun when one was bored at a musicale and stuck sitting beside one's brother, but for a potential suitor to be exposed to it was nigh on terrifying.

"He is in the yellow room, my lady," the butler continued.

"Thank you, Jonas." She touched her hair. "How do I look?"

"As pretty as always, my lady."

"You're such a flirt, Jonas," she said with a grin.

The butler's lips quirked and, having won herself a reaction, she made her way to the room, checking her appearance in a conveniently placed mirror before opening the door.

The Duke of Meacham indeed occupied the room, standing in profile at the window with his hands caught behind his back as he looked out to the London street. He was dressed impeccably, his coat tailored to frame wide shoulders and a narrow waist, his breeches displaying powerful thighs and long legs. His hair was ruthlessly groomed, perfect curls tumbling over his forehead.

He really was almost painfully pretty.

"Your Grace," she greeted. "I hope you have not been waiting long."

He turned, and the sun could not compete with his welcoming smile. "Lady Lydia. It is, as always, a delight to see you. As for the wait, I only have myself to blame, arriving unannounced as I have."

"I understand my brother may have kept you entertained."

"He did, before he was called away. I believe his betrothed required his opinion on floral arrangements."

Her lips twisted. "Harry would have been only too eager to offer his opinion. He is, unaccountably, obsessed with floristry."

"He is a complicated man, your brother."

"He is something." Moving to the lounge, she sat herself. "Won't you sit, Meacham, and I shall ring for tea."

Meacham did as she bade, arranging himself on the lounge opposite. "I enjoyed our time at the lecture."

"As did I." She placed the servant bell back on the table between them. "I found the discussion most illuminating."

"It was not only the discussion I enjoyed."

"Why, Your Grace. Do you mean you enjoy my company?"

"Always, Lady Lydia." He leaned back. "What is your opinion on the discussion?"

"I enjoyed the argument juxtaposing Wren's contributions with those of early Roman architects. I'm not certain the scholar completely made his argument, however, Oliv—Lord Roxwaithe thought perhaps the argument could have been better constructed."

Meacham's eyes flickered. "I was unaware Roxwaithe attended the lecture."

"Oh, no, he didn't." She'd discussed it with Oliver. She knew he had no particular interest in architecture, but he always listened when she had an insight or a thought and offered insightful comment, sometimes tying it to his own experience managing Roxwaithe estates.

"I see." He was silent a moment. "Will you be attending the Garfields' musicale?"

"Of course. Mama has informed me anyone who is anyone will be in attendance. I am, by all accounts, anyone, so I must attend. Tell me, Meacham, are you also anyone?"

"I am," he said.

She nodded. "I thought so," she replied with a grin.

"I hope you will allow me to escort you to the refreshments once again."

"I believe that can be arranged." Memory sparked. "Actually, I believe Roxwaithe is escorting us to the musicale."

He rubbed his lip. "Roxwaithe will be there, will he?"

"Yes. He is usually bored by the third movement, however, and will probably wander off to where all the gentlemen congregate. Wainwright is still in town, and those two will find their way to each other at most events if left to their own devices. I will be left all alone." She arched a brow.

He didn't respond.

"Or I could arrange to meet you somewhere a bit more private," she said to cover the silence. "Perhaps in the gardens? Lady Garfield always displays her statues to best advantage during a musicale. Perhaps she knows not everyone attends for the love of music."

"Perhaps." Finger rubbing his lip, he said, "You are happier than you were in Vienna."

"Of course. I am home."

"Yes." He fell silent. She resisted the urge to shift under his scrutiny. "Lady Lydia, I cannot imagine you are unaware my intentions are serious."

She would have to be blind and foolish not to realise. "I do."

"I believe we would suit admirably. I believe, with time, I would love you dearly. I should like to enter a room and know you are mine. I had every intention of asking you to marry me."

Had? "However?"

"I should like to be first in my wife's heart," he said.

Mute, she stared at him. He met her gaze levelly. That had not been what she was expecting at all. Silence stretched between them, becoming more uncomfortable with each moment that passed.

The corner of his mouth lifted ruefully. "I am surprised, actually. I never thought I should like such a thing, but I find I do."

"How do you know you would not be first in my heart?" she finally said.

"I am sorry, my dear, but it is obvious. You have strong feelings for Roxwaithe."

"I did. That is, I—"

Meacham smiled gently. "You are different around him. You are…happier. He enters a room and your gaze finds him. He is first in your thoughts. Even today, you spoke of him and his opinion, which you clearly place above all others."

"I—" she exhaled. "I am sorry."

"Don't be." His gaze shifted, becoming distant. "I should like to know how it feels. To put someone above all others. To want the best for them, always. To have their presence make me happier than anything else."

"I *am* sorry," she said.

"It's not your fault."

"It is. I like you. I do. I wanted…." She gestured helplessly.

"But you do not like me as much as you like Lord Roxwaithe."

Emotion swelled inside her. Stupid, useless emotion. "It does not matter. He thinks of me as a sister. A much younger sister."

"I have no sister, but if I did, I cannot imagine I should look at mine as he does you."

Shock stole her tongue. "I beg your pardon?"

He looked at her curiously. "He watches you. Always."

That was not why. It wasn't because he felt... He had told her.... That wasn't the reason. "It is only to display his concern." It had to be that.

"I don't know what to tell you. If I looked at a woman as he looks at you, I would not hide how I felt."

It was as if the world stopped. She stared at Meacham, unable to comprehend what he had said. Oliver had *told* her he felt nothing more than friendship, that he regarded her as a younger sister. He'd broken her heart, and then broken it again, and she had bashed her head against that wall too many times to believe...to think....

"I should go," Meacham said softly.

Thoughts a whirl, she looked at him. His expression held compassion. "Yes. Of course. I—" He didn't deserve this. Her distraction. Taking a breath, she said, "I hope we may continue our friendship."

"I, also." He paused. "If I am wrong, and you find your heart is free, I hope you would allow me to renew my suit." Bowing deeply, he gave a little smile and then departed, closing the door quietly behind him.

For the longest time, Lydia remained on the chaise, her thoughts in tatters. Meacham could not be correct. Surely. All her life, she had wanted Oliver. All her life. And he....

Shoving to her feet, she bolted from the sitting room. She didn't remember climbing the stairs or making her way into Roxegate through the shared attic. All she knew was she was suddenly before Oliver's study door, staring at the wood as she wavered on the threshold. Was he in there? Surely he would be, he was always working, and she used to sit opposite, watching him surreptitiously as he wrestled with the weight that was Roxwaithe. The real question was...would the handle turn under her hand?

She stared down at it. It was so innocuous. She used to turn it without a thought, without concern that he would shut her out. That he would deny her anything. That he didn't love her as she loved him.

She took a breath. She had to know. She had to know if Meacham was right.

The handle turned easily, the door opening silently. Oliver was seated behind his desk, his hand buried in his hair as he wrote. He was so beautiful to her, and she desperately wanted to believe Meacham, to believe that maybe.... "Oliver."

Brows drawn, he looked up. His expression lightened when he spied her. "Lydia."

He looked so happy to see her. Maybe...maybe Meacham was not wrong. "Can I?" She gestured at her chair.

Half-standing, he stopped, as if not sure how to greet her. "Yes. I would— Yes. Of course."

Closing the door behind her, she made her way to her chair. A stack of books stood on the table beside it, seeming odd and out of place. She ran her fingers over the stack, the titles jumping out at her. They were architectural tomes. More specifically, they were *her* architectural tomes. The stack she had left behind.

Oliver cleared his throat. "Was there something you wanted?"

They held no dust, and they looked as if they had last been touched not more than an hour before. For over a year they had sat here, through countless cleanings. It wasn't that they'd been forgotten. They sat in clear view of Oliver's desk, and even now his cheeks ruddied, as if he had been caught in something embarrassing. As if her books remaining here meant something.

She rested her fingers lightly on the stack. "Yes. I do want something. I want to know—" Her voice cracked. Taking a shaky breath, she continued, "I want to know how you feel."

"How I feel?"

"How you feel." She couldn't look at him. "About me."

Silence, and then, "Lydia…."

"It is only I have to know," she said in a rush. "Meacham— The Duke of Meacham came to Torrence House just now, and he said he intended to propose, but he said he would not be first in my heart. And he was right, Oliver. He was right because *you* are first in my heart. I have tried and tried to remove you, but I can't. I can't, Oliver, and then he told me…. He said…" She shook her head. "Oliver. How do you feel about me?"

He sat motionless behind his desk, a muscle working in his jaw.

Silence stretched, becoming more tense with each moment that passed, and with each moment that passed, she knew Meacham was wrong. He was so, so wrong, and Oliver wasn't going to say anything. He was going to leave her here, again, with her heart exposed and devastation in her future. It would be like when she was eighteen, except it would be worse because that would be it. She would not be able to be his friend, and she would only see him occasionally, at family gatherings and social events, and she would smile and pretend her heart wasn't breaking with each beat.

This was the end of them.

"Christ, Lydia. Don't cry."

Biting her lip, she shook her head. She couldn't stop the tears, the steady stream.

In a stride, he was by her side, his hands cupping her face. His thumbs swiped her cheeks. "Don't cry."

Closing her eyes, she gripped his biceps, wishing he felt as she did, wishing....

Lips brushed her forehead, her brow. She leant into the touch, into the moment where she could pretend....

A whisper over her cheek, her jaw, and then his lips were on hers. He kissed her softly, sweetly, and she fell into it, fell into him, in this kiss she'd always, always wanted, that made every other kiss she'd received fade into nothing, made her remember the night of her eighteenth birthday and how giddy and nervous and excited she'd been. How she'd kissed him and it had been everything she'd dreamed, everything, and then he'd pushed her away.

She pulled back. His eyes drifted open, his thumbs stroking her jaw. She searched his gaze. "Oliver?"

She saw no rejection. Instead, he lowered his head and kissed her again.

This kiss was even better. He licked at the seam of her lips and she opened, welcoming him into her. A hand slid to her neck and then covered her chest, warm and heavy against her skin, while an arm wrapped about her waist, drawing her to him, her hips against his, so close she could feel every hard inch of him against every inch of her. She'd wanted him for so long, and now he was kissing her, he was touching her, and he hadn't stopped when she gave him the opportunity. Instead, his fingers were sliding under the material of her sleeve, cupping her shoulder, warm and sure.

Lips and tongue feathered over her jaw. She arched her neck and he trailed the cord, his teeth a gentle scrape. Fingers ran over her back and her bodice came loose, gaping around her chest. She pulled her arms through, drawing his mouth back to hers as the material bunched around her waist. She pushed at his coat, and then his waistcoat, and he shucked both, bending over her, his loosened shirt gaping as he moved his lips over the top of her breasts. Hooking a finger in her corset, he said, "How do we get this loose?"

"At the back, you have to—"

He turned her around. A sharp tug, another, and her corset was loose, her chemise slipping from her shoulders as he spun her again. His throat moved as he ran his gaze over her.

Lifting her chin, she resisted the urge to cover herself. She *wanted* him to see her.

Finally, his gaze met hers. She drew her breath. His grey eyes had darkened until they were almost black, his features stark. This was how Oliver looked when lust held him in thrall.

Gaze still holding hers, he cupped her breast. Her breath caught in her throat as he shaped her flesh, his large palm warm and strong and sending fire through her veins. Her nipple tightened almost painfully and his thumb circled the puckered flesh, playing with her as his gaze burned into hers.

Wetting her lips, she barely kept her feet as her limbs turned heavy, an ache low in her belly. She couldn't tear her eyes from his, could only watch as he came closer, as he bent to her breast and replaced his thumb with his mouth.

She cried out as he tugged at her, his teeth holding her gently as his tongue lathed her. Burying her hands in his hair, she held him to her, whispering his name over and again. Suddenly, he placed an arm at her back and beneath her legs and she was in his arms as he carried her to his desk. Pushing books and papers and blotters aside, he lay her down and followed her, his bare chest—when had he lost his shirt?—against her breasts as he made a place for himself between her thighs.

"Oliver," she murmured. He growled in return, his mouth tugging at her breasts, pushing himself between her thighs. "Oliver," she murmured again, her hand stroking his hair.

He looked up at her. She curled his hair around his ear. Closing his eyes, he leaned into her touch, his hands hot on her thighs through her gown.

For a moment, the only sound in the room was their breathing, hers light and fast, his heavy.

"Lydia," he said, his voice gravel and dark.

She pulled him up to her and took his mouth with hers. He took control and it deepened into something carnal. Pushing her thighs apart, he dragged her skirts up to her waist and trailed kisses down her chest, her sternum, her belly.

Rising up on her elbows, she said uncertainly, "Oliver?"

Grey eyes met hers, full of passion, drunk with lust. "Let me. Please, Lydia. Let me."

She nodded, not really knowing what she agreed to but knowing she would refuse him nothing. Holding the back of her knees, he kissed the soft skin of her thigh and she gasped, her breath strangled in her chest. He placed a kiss higher on her thigh, his fingers digging into her flesh, then higher, and then he kissed her between her legs.

Her head thunked against the desk as sensation streaked through her. His hand covered her breast, shaping her in concert with the movements of his mouth, the licking and sucking driving her wild. Arching beneath him, she pushed into him, her hands scrambling for purchase and finding his head, his hair, the long strands she loved loose. He grunted under the tug of her fingers, his tongue finding something that made her mad, made her want, made her empty.

A finger slid inside her and she gasped loudly, the sensation almost too much. Something built, something wild and fierce, and another finger joined the first, stroking and finding something that killed her with pleasure. Her world centred on him and how he made her feel, on how much she loved him, and then everything inside her exploded.

He held her as she shuddered, whispering how glad he was he'd pleased her, how much she pleased him. Aftershocks of emotion coursed through her as he slid up her body, his mouth taking hers, and she wound herself about him, feeling drunk and dazed, and all she knew was she wanted to hold him forever.

The world came back slowly. The room was filled with the sound of their harsh breathing and a strange kind of tranquillity. Oliver's big body surrounded her, his face buried in between her shoulder and her neck and his lips brushing her skin as he panted against her, his muscles tense.

Tightening her arms around him, she held on as tight as he would let her. And she would continue to do so, for as long as he would let her.

Chapter Twelve

Hands laced over his belly, Oliver stared at the canopy over his bed. Darkness greeted him, the faintest outline of the canopy barely visible.

He deliberately did not think of Lydia.

Tomorrow would be a full day. He had a stack of paper as tall as himself to wade through, Lord Demartine had given him a new proposal for a shipping venture, and the estate in the Cotswolds needed a new roof. And he deliberately did not think of Lydia.

Exhaling, he placed his hands behind his head. Who was he trying to fool? He'd never stopped thinking of Lydia.

Earlier, she'd left with a cheeky grin and his euphoria had lasted for all of two minutes before the reality of what they had done set in. He still didn't know what had possessed him. One minute she'd been standing there, and then next she'd been in his arms and a dam, once broken, was impossible to stop. He wasn't sorry. He wasn't sorry he'd touched Lydia, kissed her, made her come. Finally, he could admit to himself he wanted her. Maybe he was too old for her, but for the moment, she had chosen him and he was finally ready to admit he had chosen her in return. From the moment he'd looked at her and realised she was a woman, he'd wanted her. He'd always been hers, and so he would enjoy it for as long as it lasted. It couldn't be forever. She would realise she didn't really want him, that there was someone younger, bolder, more amusing. Her crush would dissipate and he would let her go, never allowing her to see the broken man left behind.

The door to his bedchamber opened. A figure darted in, closing the door behind them lightning-quick. Pushing himself to his elbows, he watched as— Lydia. It had to be Lydia.

The Lydia-shaped figure moved towards his bed. The strike of a match threw light about the room. "Why is it so dark in here?" she demanded.

Of course it was Lydia. "Because it is night and I am attempting to sleep?"

Making a rude noise, she placed the candle on the fireplace mantle.

"You are where you should not be," he said mildly.

"That could be the story of my life." In a flurry of movement, she leapt upon him. Automatically, he circled his arms about her. "You're not wearing a nightshirt," she said conversationally.

"I don't." He still couldn't reconcile she was in his bedchamber.

"Are you naked?"

"I wear drawers. Lydia, why are you here?"

"I realised something," she said, her thighs hugging his hips.

"And what is that?" Hands tightening behind her back, he relished her weight upon him.

"This afternoon, you gave without taking."

Lust pooled in his groin as he recalled the taste of her, the feel of her beneath him, and the heady knowledge he was the one to afford her such pleasure. "Did I?"

"Yes." Taking his hands from her, she trapped his arms above his head and leaned over him. "I'm here to rectify that."

"How?"

"Like this," she said, and she covered his mouth with hers. Letting go of him, her hands were warm on his face as she held him still for her kiss, a perfect, hot, delicious kiss. Splaying his hands on her back, he pulled her into him, her nightgown-clad breasts flattening against his naked chest. He groaned into her as her tongue flicked at his lips, teasing him with her taste.

Sitting up, she dragged her nightgown over her head and suddenly she was naked. He barely had a moment to swallow his tongue before she leant over him, her lips hot against his neck, his shoulder, his chest. Her hair trailed through his fingers as she kissed down his chest, tonguing his nipple and lightly sucking, before kissing his stomach. Pushing at the sheets, she revealed his drawers and picked at the laces.

Oh, Christ. Christ. What was she— "Lydia?"

Fascination coloured her expression as she lifted his cock from his drawers and he hardened to stone. Holding him, she traced his length, rubbing her thumb over the tip. Lightning streaked through him and he swore.

Delighted eyes found him. "Did you like that?"

"Yes, I liked it," he ground out.

"What else do you like?"

"Lydia, you don't have to—"

"I know." Her gaze dropped to his cock. "I want to." And she leant down.

Warm breath washed over the head and then, Christ, then she *licked* him. He collapsed against his bed, sheets fisting in his hands as her eager tongue learned him. When she took him in her mouth, he just about swallowed his tongue. She was clumsy and sloppy and it was the best damn thing he'd felt in his entire life. Fire shot through him and he could feel climax storm through him, too damn quick but Christ, it was Lydia, and he better fucking warn her because he was going to come and there wasn't a goddamn thing he could do— "Lydia. Christ, Lydia, you have to stop. I'm about to—"

She released him, her fascinated gaze on his aching cock. "You're about to what?"

"Christ, I— Not in your mouth. Not this time. You— Here." Taking her hand, he wrapped her fingers around him and groaned at her touch. So good. She felt so good. He showed her how to touch him, how hard and how fast, and she watched avidly when in an embarrassingly short amount of time, he came all over her hand.

Chest heaving, he collapsed against the bed. Fuck. That was—Fuck. Fuck.

She stared at her hand. "Is this your seed?"

Barking a laugh, he threw an arm over his eyes. Only Lydia. "Yes."

Sitting up, he wiped her hand with the sheet and then kissed her, and in his kiss was gratitude and laughter and how Lydia was just so damn *Lydia* and he liked her so much.

It didn't take much for his kiss to turn from sweet to carnal. He wanted to see her fall apart again, wanted to hear her choked breath and how she moaned his name. Wrapping his arms about her, he flipped her to her back.

"Oliver, what are you doing?" she protested.

Ignoring her, he pushed her thighs open. Christ, she was glistening. Giving him pleasure had aroused her so much it had spilled onto her thighs. Hooking his arms under her knees, he covered her with his mouth. Her flavour burst on his tongue, equal parts sweet and tart, and he growled, loving he now knew her taste.

"No, Oliver, this was supposed to be for you," she moaned, her thighs hugging his ears.

He glanced up. Eyes wild with lust met his. She looked undone, and he loved he could do this to her. "This *is* for me."

Lowering his head, he set about driving her mad. Her back arched, her breasts thrust in the air. Reaching up, he covered them, her pebble-hard nipples stabbing his palms. Her thighs squeezed his head as she gasped and moaned, her head thrashing. Abandoning her breasts, he took hold of them and forced her open, holding her still for his lips and tongue. She was soft and wet and hot and he wanted inside her so badly. He ground his hips into the bedsheets, so damn hard even though she'd just made him come.

Remembering how it had driven her wild that afternoon, he licked and sucked at her bud and, then, sank a finger inside her. She was tight and even hotter and wetter and he added another, finding that place inside her that made her scream.

Pushing herself into him, her mouth opened on a silent scream as she erupted, squeezing his fingers as she came and flooding him with more of her sweet-tart flavour. He doubled his efforts and she bucked again, her body rigid as pleasure wracked her.

"Stop. Oliver, stop. It's too much," she gasped, pushing at his head.

With one last kiss, he reluctantly pulled away. Wiping his mouth, he placed a kiss on her belly, her sternum, her breast, before taking her lips. She kissed him back, her arms winding about him as her hands tightened in his hair.

He kissed her again, and then again, and then, with a sigh, he settled on his back beside her. She lay next to him, dazed, and he smirked at the canopy. He had done that. He had pleasured Lydia Torrence into silence.

After a while, she said, "We should do that again."

Unable to stop his grin, he turned to her. "Ready whenever you are."

"Now?"

"Now." Leaning over her, he applied himself to tasting every single inch of her skin.

***

OLIVER LIGHTLY DRAGGED HIS fingertips over Lydia's back. She lay on her front, her cheek resting on her folded hands with her eyes closed. The sheet pooled around their hips, the light from the flickering candle picking out hills and valleys. Her skin was soft and warm, and he'd never felt such contentment as he did right at this moment.

"You're very good at this."

His cheeks heated. What the bloody hell could he say to that? He couldn't— "How would you know?"

"It's good that you practiced," she continued, ignoring him. "I shall only have to educate you slightly."

Jealously was a petty emotion and he would not allow it to control him. "Who did you practice with?"

Her eyes opened. "What does it matter? None were you."

He supposed, but.... "Who?"

"How many did you practice with?" she countered.

"What?"

"How. Many. Did y*ou*. Pract—"

His face felt like it was on fire. "I'm not discussing this with you."

"Ha! It's different now it's on the other foot." Grinning, she propped herself on an elbow, her red-gold hair spilling over his pillows. "How many?"

"Enough to know what I'm doing." He closed his eyes briefly. "I wish I'd waited."

She stilled. "Pardon?"

"I wish this was new to me. That I only knew you." He didn't begrudge any of the women he'd been with—not that there had been many—but he wished he'd realised Lydia was the only one he wanted. "How did you know what to do?" Her eyes were soft and...wet? Christ, what had he said? "Lydia?"

Taking a shuddering breath, she said, "Know what to do what?"

"When we—" He gestured vaguely, feeling awkward as hell.

"Ah. *When* we." She settled into his side. "Harry and George don't hide things nearly as well as they think they do. They have the most interesting books stashed under their beds."

"And that is where you learnt this?"

"They had pictures, Oliver. If you think Violet and I didn't study those books thoroughly, I will have to disappoint you."

"I am not disappointed. At all." He brushed his lips over the top of her head, his hair falling forward at the move.

She tugged at the strand before he could pull back. "I love this."

"My hair?"

She nodded, watching the strands fall from her fingers. "More and more of it would fall about your face as the day progressed, and you would shove it back impatiently, not even aware you did so."

"You chewed on the end of your hair."

Hazel eyes flew to his, a question in their depths.

"When you concentrated," he clarified. "But then, you stopped doing it and you'd brush your lips with the ends instead."

"That was Miss Chisholm. She was quite aghast at the habit and set about correcting it." She placed the ends of his hair against her lips. "I've not seen it fully down before. It's quite long."

"Below my shoulders."

"Why is it so long? Tis not the fashion."

He'd never actually said it out loud. "My father hated it."

It sounded petty and small, but words couldn't come close to conveying the maelstrom that swirled within him. It had been his one small rebellion. His father had ruthlessly controlled every aspect of his appearance, and the moment his hair had touched his ears, his father had ordered it cut. Then, his father had died.

Lydia ran her fingers gently over the beard on his chin. "And this?"

"Same as my hair." Twice a day he'd been compelled to shave, his father inspecting his jaw.

Cupping his cheek, she placed a kiss on his chin. "I'm sorry."

"For what?"

"That your father was horrible."

He blinked. Christ. His father *was* horrible. He'd never thought of it that way, but he had been a terrible father. Wrapping his arms about her, he hugged her tight. She was everything to him. "You are so beautiful."

Her gaze flickered. "Oh. Thank you."

"No, I—" He wasn't explaining it well. He didn't mean— "*You* are beautiful. All of you. Every part of you. Your mind. Your compassion. That you say such a thing as my father was horrible and you are right. He *was* horrible. You say things and you make me think of it a different way, and I.... You are beautiful."

It still didn't explain enough, didn't convey what she meant to him, how she made him better, how she was the best person he knew. The one whose opinion, whose insights, he most wanted. The first person he wanted to discuss anything with, the first person he thought of each morning, the last he thought of each night, and how when she was on the Continent he'd missed her. He'd missed her so much.

She bit her lip, her eyes wet.

"You're not—I didn't—Don't cry."

"I'm not," she said as a tear slipped over her cheek.

He captured it with his thumb. "Lydia—"

Her hand wrapped around his, her fingers caressing his palm. "You mean everything to me."

The lump in his throat made it difficult to swallow. Bringing her hand to his lips, he brushed a kiss over her fingers.

"Don't let me fall asleep," she whispered.

"I won't." He stroked her hair as she settled against him, her fingers smoothing the smattering of hair on his chest, and he tried not to think about how perfectly she fit by his side. All night he held her, and neither of them fell asleep.

Chapter Thirteen

Music followed Lydia as she made her way from the ballroom. The Sandersons' ball had attracted those members of society still in London and was a fairly packed affair, though nowhere near the heights of a London in the full swing of the season. She offered distracted smiles to those revellers who wandered the same halls she did, her focus wholly on reaching her destination with as little notice as possible.

Turning a corner into a hall devoid of people, she abandoned any pretention to decorum, lifted her skirts, and ran. Excitement thrummed in her veins and a wild laugh bubbled inside her as she raced through the halls.

The orangery lit up with lightning, casting long shadows as thunder rumbled and, deep amongst the greenery, she found him. Oliver stood with his back to her, hands laced loosely behind him. She took a moment to soak him in. Broad shoulders. Slim hips. Long legs. His hair gathered into a knot at his nape, ruthlessly contained at the minute but it would take so little to ruin that precision. To ruin him.

Lust punched her. Wetting her lips, she knew she could give in to that lust, touch him as she'd always wanted to touch him, and he would welcome her. She revelled in that knowledge.

"Oliver." He turned, and his expression when he saw her— his eyes alight, his lips curving into a glorious smile—

She threw herself at him. As always, he was surprised by her exuberance but surprise did not stop him from returning her kiss, wrapping his arms around her and hauling her close. He kissed her as if he hadn't done so in months, though it had been last night she'd again crept to his bedchamber and they'd pleasured each other in his bed. For almost a week, she had shared his bed, and it had been the best week of her life. They had not yet crossed the final line in their passion, but she had no wish to endure the rumours that would follow a baby born less than nine months from their wedding, and she was certain Oliver felt the same.

Resting his cheek against her hair, he gathered her close, his body hard and ready against her but holding her with such tenderness.

Rubbing her lips against his jaw, she said, "Hello."

"Hello." His arms tightened about her. "Is the door shut?"

"I don't know." Eyes drifting closed, she breathed him in, that scent that was rosemary and leather and him.

Setting her from him, concern creased his brow. "We cannot be reckless."

"How is this reckless?" Another low rumble of thunder. The evening was yet dry though rain threatened with every peal. "Who would venture this far on such an evening?"

"Plenty," he said darkly.

She bit her lip. "I wanted to see you, Oliver."

Expression softening, he said, "And I, you."

Contentment flowing through her, she traced his brow. "How was your day?"

"Tolerable," he said. "The stack of paper never seems to decrease."

She hummed, ghosting her fingers over his cheek, the soft bristles of his beard playing along her skin.

"What did you do?" he asked, leaning into her touch.

"Violet and I went shopping, though that was mostly for Violet." His lips were so soft, and she loved that she knew that, she loved touching him, and she loved that he let her.

"So you bought nothing?"

"Perhaps I bought some ribbon. And a pelisse. And maybe a bonnet." She inhaled sharply as he nipped at her skin. "I may have also ordered a dress."

"Bad Lydia." His tongue flicked against the abused flesh.

She gasped. With a feral grin, he took her hand and led her to a day bed, hauling her into his lap. Eagerly she went, pulling her skirts up to straddle him, and hands tugged at her bodice. The fabric fell away easily, as easily as his jacket, his waistcoat, the cravat from his neck. Tugging his shirt from his pants, she dug her fingers into warm flesh as she rocked against him, aching. He grunted, his mouth sucking at her neck, and his hand covered her breast, rubbed her nipple. Skin on fire, she arched against him.

"You feel so good," he ground out. She moaned in agreement, trying to get closer, wanting everything, wanting him. Lightning crashed to light Oliver's face, his grey eyes dark with lust. Taking the lobe of his ear between her teeth, she bit gently and soothed with her tongue, bit and soothed. Muscles suddenly tense, he was still under her touch. Smoothing her hands over his shoulders, she nuzzled his neck, ran her tongue over his jaw.

Jerking back, he grabbed her upper arms. "Lydia."

His voice was like a dash of cold water, cutting through her lust. "What?" She swallowed, her tongue thick. "What is it?"

"Did you shut the door?"

She couldn't— Shaking herself, she tried to focus. "Yes."

"Did you lock it?" he said, his expression hard.

Hunching her shoulders, she pulled her bodice into place, of a sudden feeling horribly exposed. "I don't think there was a lock."

He cursed.

She flinched. "What is it?"

"I saw someone," he said grimly.

"What do you mean?"

"A face. Over there."

"So?"

"What do you mean, 'so'? I saw a face. Someone could have seen us, Lydia."

"What does it matter?"

"Of course it matters!" He exhaled harshly. "It matters, Lydia," he said in a more measured tone. "If we're seen, your options will narrow to one."

"But you are my option. My only option."

Jaw working, he stared at her.

"Oliver?"

Shooting to his feet, he started to pace. "You don't know what you want."

She rose, too. "Don't tell me what I want."

"You're too young—"

"Damnation, Oliver!" Well, at least she'd shocked him to silence. "I am not too young. I am twenty years old, well past the age most women wed. I have travelled the Continent. I have refused numerous offers. I know my mind and I know what I want. I want you. I have *always* wanted you."

He shook his head.

Unbelievable. He— Why couldn't he get it through his thick skull? "Do you not believe me?"

"You don't know what you want. You've not.... Lydia, you haven't the experience. You fixated on me, and I have taken shameless advantage. You don't want me. You just think have no other option."

"Oliver," she said in a small voice. "Do you not believe I want you?"

"I believe you think you want me," he said wearily. "There are other men, Lydia. Better men. Younger men. This is temporary."

He was so *infuriating*. "Of course I want you, Oliver. I've always wanted you."

Jaw set, he turned his head.

"No." Grabbing his face, she forced him to look at her. "I love you."

His gaze slid from hers.

She wanted to scream. She wanted to beat at him, to force him to believe her, to make him as angry as she was with him. How dare he discount her feelings? How dare he dictate to her how she felt? He had no clue, not one. All her life, she'd known it was him she'd wanted. All. Her. Life. She shouldn't have to convince him of this. Everyone knew she wanted him. Even *Seraphina Waller-Mitchell* knew. He was—

Exhaling, she forced herself to calm. She would not deal with this now. She was too angry and she would say something she would regret. "I think we should return to the ballroom," she said evenly.

Uncertainty troubled his expression, but she found she didn't much care to explain her sudden change in mood. "I will return to Roxegate. You should find your mother."

"And what will that accomplish?"

He still regarded her warily. "I don't know, but Lady Demartine will fix it. She's good at fixing disasters."

Her heart cracked. "This is a disaster?"

"No. No, of course not. Lydia...." Licking his lips, he ran his hand over his head, fingers snagging in the loose strands. She had pulled those strands free. When they were behaving disastrously.

"I see." Numbness coated her. "You should go to Roxegate. I will find my mother."

"Lydia—"

"No," she said sharply.

Jaw working, he stared at her.

Suddenly, she was tired. So tired. Presenting her back, she said, "Please button me."

Silently, he did as she bade and they were silent as they righted themselves.

"I will go first," she said.

"Lydia...."

Ignoring him, she left the orangery. Turning a corner, she leant against a wall and sagged. How could she argue in the face of such belief? She had never wavered, and yet still he disbelieved her, thought her silly and young and unable to make a decision. How could he think such of her?

Wrapping her arms about her middle, she pressed hard. It hurt so much he didn't *know* her, he didn't *trust* her. How could she want someone who didn't trust her, trust she knew her own mind and had the courage of her convictions?

Exhaling, she rubbed her brows. This wasn't going to be solved now. Now, she had to re-enter the ballroom and pretend all was well. Pushing away from the wall, she started down the hall only to stop in surprise.

Ahead, arguing in low tones, were Seraphina Waller-Mitchell and Stephen Farlisle.

They were close, barely half a foot apart, and Seraphina looked…distraught. Never had Lydia seen such an expression on the other woman's face before. She didn't even know Seraphina could display any emotion bar smug superiority. Stephen wore anger and a faint air of disappointment. He spoke urgently, and then he made to leave. Seraphina captured his arm but he shook her off and, with a final look, left.

Lydia didn't know what to do. The only way back to the ballroom was to pass by Seraphina. The other woman looked miserable, her hands cradling her elbows as she stared at the floor.

There was nothing for it. She would have to pass her.

Seraphina looked up as Lydia approached and her expression changed, becoming the mocking smirk society knew. "Well, well, if it isn't Lydia Torrence. Whatever are you doing here, Lydia Torrence?" Her tone held its usual mocking edge, but underlying it was a thread of tears.

Lydia squared her shoulders. "Are you crying?"

Seraphina started, and then her chin raised mulishly. "Why are you wandering the halls, or perhaps I can guess? However, I don't really need to. I know it has to do with Lord Roxwaithe."

Unease slithered down her spine. "You don't know anything."

"I know you were in the orangery. I know you were...close."

The face. Oliver's conviction they were seen. "Do you?"

"It would be unfortunate if that knowledge were to become more widely known."

Something inside her broke. First Oliver's obstinacy and now Seraphina Waller-Mitchell's spite. "You know what, Seraphina? I don't care. Tell my family. Tell everyone. Do you think I care what other people think? Do you think I care what *you* think?"

Slowly the smirk faded from Seraphina's expression. "You don't?"

Lydia kept Seraphina's gaze, refused to give her surcease.

The other woman swallowed. "Why don't you?"

"Because...." Leaning close, she lowered her tone, so Seraphina knew just how much she *meant* it. "I don't like you."

Stricken, Seraphina Waller-Mitchell stared at her. Lydia walked off, not caring how Seraphina would react next. She didn't care. She had her family and, damnation, she had Oliver. He was buffle-headed and wrong, but she'd be *damned* if he destroyed them because of some fool-headed notion.

Stopping, she took a shuddering breath. She'd just stood up to Seraphina Waller-Mitchell. She'd just looked her direct in the eye and told her she didn't like her. Well. Wasn't this a red-letter evening.

Clasping her hands together, she closed her eyes. The problem of Oliver's disbelief would be solved. She would come up with a plan and she would make it work. She loved him too much not to and, damnation, she knew he loved her in return. She would make him see, even if it took her forever. So determined, she started again toward the ballroom.

Tomorrow. She would know what to do tomorrow.

Chapter Fourteen

OLIVER STARED AT THE paper in his hand. The report on the Roxwaithe shipping concern had blurred into an unrecognisable splotch of ink on paper. A light breeze ran over his skin from the open window, sounds of everyday life drifting in, and he was vaguely aware of Rajitha scratching away at his desk. It was a day, an ordinary day.

"Rajitha," he said suddenly.

The secretary looked up, uncharacteristically displaying his surprise.

"I have no need of you this afternoon," Oliver said. "You may take your leave."

"My lord?" his secretary queried, clearly confused by the unusual dismissal.

"Thank you, Rajitha."

The secretary opened his mouth as if to argue but instead, without a word, he packed his desk, gathering papers, inkwell and pen. With a final bow, he departed.

Left alone, Oliver gave up any pretence at work. Leaning back in his chair, he dug the heels of his hands into his eyes. Christ. What was he going to do? This...whatever it was with Lydia, he hadn't meant for it to go so far. Seeing an opportunity, he'd selfishly taken what he'd wanted without any thought to consequence or how he'd ruined her options. He was an idiot and a fool, and it didn't matter it was the happiest he'd ever been, he should have been stronger for her. He should have resisted, but he'd been resisting for so long. He'd been weary so he'd broken, and now he'd broken them.

The study door banged open. His brother stormed in, his expression tight with fury. "What did you do?"

Oliver's spine snapped straight. "I'll thank you to lower your voice."

"I shall clarify," Stephen said tightly. "What did you do to Lydia Torrence?"

A roaring started in his head, his blood turning cold. "What do you mean? Is she hurt?"

"Christ, Oliver, what were you thinking?" Stephen continued, oblivious to the panic coursing through Oliver.

"Stephen. Is. She. Hurt?" he ground out, fear turning his voice to gravel.

Stephen's gaze snapped to him. "No. Not physically, however it was a damn near thing. You're lucky the rumour didn't spread."

She was unhurt. Relief lasted but a moment before dread pooled in his stomach. "What rumour?"

"That you and Lydia...." The skin of Stephen cheekbones turned ruddy. "That you...."

"What?"

"Don't make me say it." Exhaling, he said reluctantly, "That you and she were...caught."

"Caught?"

"Bloody hell, man, what do you think I mean? Caught!"

The flash of lightning. The pale face. Lydia warm in his lap, her lips smiling against his neck. "We were caught?"

Stephen braced his hands on the back of the chair before Oliver's desk. "You mean there was something you could have been caught doing?"

Oliver's neck burned. Setting his jaw, he stared Stephen down. He wasn't going to be shamed by his younger brother. "It is none of your concern."

"Of course it's my bloody concern. Lydia is like a sister to me. Do you think you're the only one with ties to the Torrences?" He ran a hand through his short blond hair. "What were you thinking, Oliver?"

Clearly, he hadn't been thinking. He'd seen an opportunity and he'd taken it, even though he knew the risks, even though he knew it was temporary. He'd done it, and he had no excuse.

Stephen shook his head. "Couldn't you have just married her first?"

Oliver's gaze jerked to his brother. "What?"

"We wouldn't be in this mess now. I wouldn't have had to—" He swallowed, looked away.

His brother looked miserable. He opened his mouth to ask, but that had never been their relationship. Instead, he said, "I can't marry her."

Stephen passed his hand over his eyes wearily. "Not this again."

"I am too old for her."

"You know she is in love with you."

"She is not. Not really."

Stephen looked to the heavens. "Fine. Let us say, for the sake of argument, she is not in love with you. What about you?"

Crossing his arms, he said, "What about me?"

"You are hers. You've always been hers. You've been on hold, waiting for her. Everyone knows it, but for some reason you refuse to acknowledge it. You won't just bloody *admit* it." He exhaled. "I am tired of this, brother. I am tired of being your heir. Just marry Lydia, unite our families officially, and set about the business of disinheriting me. You cannot play with her, Oliver."

"I am not playing with her."

"No, I know. This is deadly serious." Exhaling again, his brother rubbed his hand over his face.

Oliver dug his fingers into his biceps. He thought of Lydia. He thought of her sitting in his study, reading book after book. He thought of her opinions, freely given and the ones he most wanted. He thought of her grin, her laugh, the way she made him laugh. He thought of how she made him feel, how happy she made him. He thought of how happy he seemed to make her.

"I love her," he said.

Stephen snorted. "Everyone knows that."

"I *love* her." He'd never admitted it. Not to anyone. Not even to himself. "I don't know what to do.

Stephen rolled his eyes. "*Marry* her."

He shook his head. "She deserves more."

"It doesn't matter what you think she deserves. She wants *you*."

"She only thinks she does. She's too young to know what she wants."

Stephen laughed shortly. "She's known what she's wanted since she was a girl. Why are you so convinced she doesn't know her own mind?"

He didn't look at his brother, staring at the blotter on his desk. The leather was scuffed in the top right hand corner, a mishap when he was a boy. His father had not been pleased.

Silence stretched, and he filled it with all the reasons why he shouldn't marry Lydia...and all the reasons he should.

"I don't want to study the occult," Stephen said suddenly.

Oliver blinked. "Pardon?"

"I don't want to study the occult." Expression mulish, Stephen couldn't quite disguise the undercurrent of unease. "I wanted money."

"I beg your pardon?" Oliver said.

"I knew you wouldn't give me funds outright, not if I told you what they were really for, so...." Jaw set, he shrugged. "I lied."

"You lied."

"Yes."

The clock ticked on the mantle, loud in the silence of the study.

"Why?" Oliver finally asked.

"It's worked before."

He took a slow, steadying breath. "I see. So what was your plan to secure funds...." Just like that, he knew. Because Stephen *had* done it before. "You would feign interest in a plan even an idiot would know was doomed to failure. Once I'd refused to release your funds, you would wait a few weeks and then apply again, this time with much more reasonable request."

"And you would agree," Stephen said.

Numb, Oliver nodded. "What did you want it for this time?"

Stephen worked his jaw. "I wanted to start a football team."

"A football team."

"For workhouse lads. It was to have been a charitable foundation to improve their.... We thought to encourage them to attend the parish school with a certain degree of attendance, have it as a requirement to play in the competition— I wanted to help. I do not have many skills, but I know football and—" A muscle ticked in Stephen's jaw. "I wanted money for a football team."

"So, you lied so you could start a charity."

"Yes, Oliver. I lied to start a charity."

Eyeing his brother, he rubbed a hand over his chin. Stephen stared back at him without expression, not giving even a hint as to what he was thinking.

"Did you not think to talk to me about this?" Oliver asked. "Did you not think I would not want to help? Christ, Stephen, if not because you're my brother, but because it would be the decent thing to do?"

"You have never helped before."

He stared at him in disbelief. "It is *all* I do."

"Not without a goddamn argument!" Stephen lowered his tone. "You never support me. You don't believe I have any idea how to handle finances or what might be best for me. Christ. Is it any wonder you won't believe Lydia either?"

"Do not bring her into this," Oliver said dangerously.

"Why not? You behave in the exact same way with both of us."

"Lydia didn't attempt to extort *money* from me."

"No. She just wanted your heart, but you won't allow her, will you? You'd rather play us all, puppets tangled in your strings, begging for scraps."

"Don't presume you know my mind, brother," he said, and he heard their father in his tone.

"Yes. Of course. My lord," Stephen said coldly.

Before he could respond, the door to the study opened. Annoyed at the interruption, he prepared to lambast whoever stepped through.

Standing there, with his hand in Alexandra Torrence's, was Maxim.

Oliver blinked. No. It couldn't be. His youngest brother was dead. He'd died years ago. He couldn't be standing on the threshold of Roxegate's study, looking older and weathered and....

The man who couldn't be Maxim moved further into the room. His hair was ragged, his skin tanned, and he wore rough clothing. He was huge, at least a foot taller than the Maxim of Oliver's memory, and broad. His brother had been skinny as a rake, but he'd had the promise of that width in his bony shoulders.

The man looked at them uncertainly, and then he glanced at Alexandra. Squeezing his arm, she seemed to silently say something to him and he saw the man square his shoulders, as if the look they'd shared had given him resolve. Alexandra and his brother had always been like that, as if they were connected in a way only the two of them could understand.

"I presume we have arrived ahead of the letter," the man finally said.

The words were spoken in a deeper and rougher voice but unmistakeably *Maxim's* voice. His brother, who had been fifteen when last he'd seen him, who had been presumed dead, had instead grown into a man.

Oliver sat frozen behind his desk. Christ. It *was* Maxim. He didn't know how to react. Stephen appeared as shell-shocked as he. His brother—*his middle brother*—wiped his hand over his mouth as he stared, his face pale.

Alexandra turned to Maxim and he leant down as she whispered something. Shaking his head, he whispered something back and they seemed to have an argument before reaching a consensus. They both turned to regard Oliver and Stephen.

Alexandra smiled nervously. "Maxim would like me to stay, if that's agreeable to you both."

Her voice broke his stasis and Oliver shot to his feet. "Of course you may remain. You should— Please. Both of you sit." He moved to the chair before the fireplace and gestured to the chaise. They both sat, Maxim's hand in Alexandra's lap. Stephen still stood by Oliver's desk, silent and pale.

Oliver stared at their clasped hands. "Where have you been?" he asked Maxim.

"Lately, Waithe Hall. Alexandra found me there." He gave her a slight smile.

She smiled back, and he saw between them the love their friendship had always promised. Unable to think about that, he concentrated on his returned brother. "And before?"

"The Americas," he said. "Boston. After the shipwreck, after I had recovered from my injuries, I was employed as a servant. At first, I had no memory of who I was, but eventually I recalled enough to remember my home was in England. I bought passage on a ship as a shiphand. Sometime after I arrived in

London, I saw the Roxwaithe carriage and I...remembered."

Oliver locked his jaw. "But you did not come to us."

Uncertainty leant youth to his features and, in that moment, Oliver saw his fifteen-year-old brother. Inhaling sharply, he fought the pressure behind his eyes.

"I could not," Maxim said softly. "Not after what Father had said."

"What did Father say?"

All three of them looked at Stephen. He still stood by Oliver's desk, was still pale. "What did Father say?" Stephen repeated.

Maxim glanced again at Alexandra, who smiled reassuringly. "He said not to return. He said my shame was too great."

"What shame?" Stephen asked.

Maxim shook his head.

"What shame?" he pressed.

Seeing his youngest brother's discomfort, Oliver said, "Perhaps we should—"

"No," Stephen said sharply. "What shame?"

"Stephen," Oliver said. "Our brother has just returned. How does this matter?"

"It matters!" he shouted. "It bloody matters. Maxim *died*, Oliver. He died and now he's back and—" He choked up and turned away, shoulders shaking.

Feeling completely useless, Oliver stared at his brother. His middle brother. Because Maxim had returned.

"Father said he would disown me," Maxim answered. "Because I was sent down from Eton for cheating, but I didn't cheat. I paid someone to write my assignments, but I dictated every word, and the reason I did that— The reason— I can't—" He exhaled slowly. Alexandra squeezed his hand and he glanced at her quickly, seeming to take comfort from her. "I can't read," he said.

"You *can* read," Alexandra said fiercely.

"But not well." He gave her a little smile. "Not well."

"Perhaps not, but we are seeking help." She looked between Oliver and Stephen. "George will know of a treatment, and if he doesn't, he will know someone who can." She scowled. "Maxim is *not* stupid."

"Of course not," Oliver said.

Alexandra nodded, her expression still fierce.

Suddenly, he thought of Lydia. He thought of her defending him as Alexandra did his brother, and he wanted her here. She should be here. His life was hers, and she should be present for every moment of it, especially the extraordinary ones. She should be here.

But she wasn't and it was his own damn fault. "This is why you and Father fought?" he asked, focussing on his brother.

Maxim nodded. "He said I should not return home. I said I would become a shiphand on a Roxwaithe ship, and he did not disagree, so I did. I.... It was a bull-headed move."

Stephen made a rude noise. "Father was the bull-headed one."

"He was wrong," Oliver said. "Father was wrong. You should never have been made to feel you should have left, and that you were ever not welcome when you returned. You need never be unsure of your welcome, Maxim. You are always welcome." He shook his head. "Maxim. You are *alive*."

The corner of his youngest brother's lip twitched. "I am."

Oliver started to laugh. A smile stole across Maxim's face, and even Stephen reluctantly smiled. Alexandra beamed, looking between the three of them.

Christ. The *three* of them.

And in the midst of it all, as he marvelled over the return of his brother, all he wanted was to tell Lydia.

Chapter Fifteen

Lydia stared down at the embroidery in her hands. She hardly knew what she was sewing, but she was sure she was making a muddle of it. It was impossible to keep her focus, when Maxim Farlisle had returned from the dead.

Across the room, Alexandra sat beside their mother, her own embroidery lying forgotten in her lap. Her gaze was glued to the door, her attention clearly in the study with their father and Maxim.

It had been over a week since Alexandra had returned from Bentley Close clutching the hand of the boy they had all believed dead. Her father had paled. Her mother had cried. Harry hadn't known what to say, which was proof enough of his incredulity. Tessa had, of course, never known Maxim and had to be introduced, while letters were written to both George and Michael. As for Lydia.... Her first thought had been for Oliver.

Maxim himself, however, was now a man fully grown and, from the little Alexandra had told them, had experienced a myriad of trouble in his time away. Lost memories, servitude, a harrowing journey back to England, not to mention the shipwreck that had started it all. Then, to add to their shock, Alexandra had announced their intent to marry, practically glowing with happiness.

Frowning, Lydia stabbed at the fabric.

Once it learned of Maxim's return, society had been in an uproar. A horde had descended upon Roxegate and, when denied admittance, had turned their attention to Torrence House. All were aware of the bond between the Torrences and the Farlisles, and when news had broken of Alexandra's engagement to Maxim, the frenzy had intensified. It was such now Lydia could not step from the house without being accosted. Violet had attempted to brave the fray, but after fighting through the throng, she'd emerged white-faced in the entrance of Torrence House and had declared she would not attempt again until the fever had died down.

"What is taking so long?" Alexandra burst out. Her sister now sat with arms crossed over her stomach, her foot tapping the floor wildly.

"It will take as long as it takes," their mother said calmly.

"But they have been in there for an hour! What can they possibly be talking about?"

"The weather?" Lydia offered.

Alexandra shot her a dirty look. "That is not helpful."

Their mother frowned. "Don't tease your sister, Lydia. Alexandra, you know they are discussing the legalities of Maxim's return. Your father was closeted for over a day with Roxwaithe discussing the particulars earlier this week and that has barely scratched the surface. If you wish to marry him, we must ensure he is again legally recognised as Lord Maxim Farlisle."

At the mention of Oliver, Lydia stared hard at her embroidery.

Alexandra sighed. "I know, Mama, it is only…. It is difficult to be patient. I have been eleven years without him."

Their mother's expression softened. "I understand, dear. Your father is doing everything he can as quickly as he can."

Lydia bit her lip as the cloth before her blurred. How did Oliver feel about his brother's return? He would be stoic and logical and methodical, but no one would think to ask how he felt. He would no doubt be alone in his study, working through the particulars of returning his brother to society, and no one was there to hug him and tell him it was all right to feel whatever he was feeling, and to let him talk, and vent, and whatever else he needed to do. Maxim's return had rocked her own family, she could only imagine how Oliver's had fared. He and Stephen were not close, and she held little hope Maxim's return had magically reconciled them. It would have made a complex situation even more so, and Oliver would have no one to talk to, no one he could share any fears or trepidations, or express frustration or anger, or joy, or happiness, or whatever he felt. He had no one.

No one but her.

She stood. Both Alexandra and their mother looked at her in surprise. Awkwardly, she said, "I, um…I am going to my chamber."

"At this hour?" their mother asked.

She nodded. "Yes," she said unnecessarily. "I might take a tray for dinner. I—I can feel a headache coming." *Brilliant, Lydia. Just brilliant.*

Her mother did not look convinced, but she didn't protest when Lydia left the sitting room. Instead of going to her chamber, however, she climbed the stairs to the attic. In moments she was through to the Roxegate side, and as she had a thousand times before, she made the journey to Oliver's study.

The door was closed. She stared at it. Should she tentatively knock, boldly enter, or just leave well enough alone and return home?

Be damned to it all. Enough with this dithering. Boldly entering it was.

Jerking the door open, she strode into the study. Oliver stood by the window, staring out on the throng of journalists and gawkers that had taken residence on the street. At her entrance, he turned and, brows drawn, he stared at her.

She stared back. Now that she stood before him, she could only remember the flash of lightning across his face, his expression as he didn't believe her.

Silence stretched between them.

Finally, she remembered why she'd come. He looked tired, and his hair was falling from where it was gathered at his nape. He'd removed his jacket and his waistcoat was half undone. She took a step toward him. "Oliver, I— Your brother. Maxim. How are y—"

In an explosion of movement, he strode toward her and gathered her to him, his arms around her tight. He was tense, his muscles jumping. Tentatively, she stroked his back. "Oliver?"

Burying his face in her neck, he shuddered against her.

Stroking his hair, she brushed her lips against his temple. "Oliver," she murmured.

He didn't respond, his big body curling around hers. She felt wetness against her skin, and she bit her lip as she blinked away her own tears.

With a shuddering breath, he pulled back, and wet grey eyes searched hers. "He's returned, Lydia."

"I know." She rubbed his back, her heart aching at his bewilderment.

"My brother isn't dead. He didn't die. He's.... Lydia, Maxim is alive."

"Shh. I know."

"I've had to apply to the crown, and see our solicitors, and your father has helped, but.... Lydia. Maxim is alive." Gaze sharpening, he cupped her face. "I love you. I am in love with you. I'm sorry I ever made you think I was not."

Every part of her froze. Like a fool, she stared at him. She couldn't think. Everything seemed muddled and upside down and she couldn't *think*.

"I know this is most likely a shock," he continued, seemingly unaware he'd just upended her whole world. "It's only I don't want to waste any more time."

She shook her head. He couldn't be saying this to her. "Why?" she managed.

"Maxim came home," he said, his thumb stroking her cheek. "We thought he was dead, and he came *home*. He— I—" He shook his head. "I've been doing everything I can to legally bring him back, and your father's been here, and Alexandra, and even your mother came once, and all I could think was I wanted *you*. I wanted to tell you he'd returned, and I couldn't— No one knows me as you do. I am myself around you. I can tell you anything, and your opinion matters to me, the only one that matters, and I hadn't told you he'd returned." He swallowed. "Lydia, you should have been here, and you weren't because I'm an idiot."

Violently, she shook her head in protest.

"I am. I should have admitted long ago how I felt. I hurt you." His thumb rubbed away a tear on her cheek.

A hundred remembered hurts slid through her. His rejection when she was eighteen. His insistence he only felt friendship. His resentment of Meacham as her suitor. His behaviour at the Sandersons' ball. "You *did* hurt me."

"I know."

"You made me think I was imagining everything. I had to go to the Continent to recover. You made me leave my family, my friends."

"I know."

She hit his chest. "You hurt me, Oliver."

"I know." Sorrow and regret in his grey eyes, he stood under her abuse. "I'll spend the rest of my life proving how sorry I am."

Half-heartedly, she hit his chest again and then she exhaled shakily. "I suppose I can forgive you. Your brother just returned from the dead, after all."

A pause. "I would be forever grateful."

"You should be. I am being very magnanimous."

"You are," he said gravely.

Wrapping her arms about his waist, she rested her forehead on his shoulder. His arms encircled her hesitantly, as if he were still unsure of her, and so she said, "I love you, too."

He stilled. "You don't have to say it because I did."

"I'm not." She pulled back to meet his troubled gaze. "Oliver, I'm not."

"How can you be sure?"

Confusion drew her brows. "Sure that I'm not saying it because you did?"

"No. That you love me." His gaze slid from hers. "Lydia, you decided you wanted to marry me when you were a child. How do you *know*?"

Oh. The poor, sweet, *dense* man. "I love you, Oliver. I love your compassion." She kissed his brow. "Your determination." She kissed his other brow. "Your wit. Your candour. The way you are with me. The way you are with everyone else. I love that you listen to me. That you look at me as if I'm the only person in the room. That you hold my opinion so highly, and that you want to share yourself with me." Holding his face, she held his gaze. "I love *you*, Oliver. I always have."

Closing his eyes, he leaned into her touch. "Lydia...."

"You know I love you." She brushed his lips with hers. "You *know* it."

"You love me?"

The vulnerability in his voice just about broke her. "You know I do."

He opened his eyes and she drowned in grey. "I do."

Tossing her head, she said, "Of course you know. I've never been afraid of saying it, unlike some."

He started to laugh. Holding her to him, he buried his face in her neck. "I love you," he said, his words muffled against her skin.

"I love you, too." And he, finally, didn't protest.

She didn't know how long they stood in each other's embrace but slowly, as it always did, lust and passion stirred. The air thickened between them. Her skin tingled, and she wanted to have his taste in her mouth. How utterly inappropriate. He had sweetly told her of his love and now all she wanted was to make him groan as he lost himself in her.

"Lydia," he said thickly.

Raising her head, she looked at him. Lust drew his features, his colour high.

She licked her lips.

His gaze zeroed on the movement. "Lydia," he said again with a voice full of gravel. "Do you wish to enter our marriage bed a virgin?"

Heat streaked through her, tightening her nipples and gathering low in her belly. Slowly, she shook her head.

His eyes darkened. Untangling himself from her, he strode to the door and, deliberately, turned the lock. She watched him, unable to tear her gaze from the shape of his shoulders, the muscles moving beneath the fine lawn of his shirt.

He returned to her and they stared at each other. "Are we to wed?" she asked.

"Yes." His gaze devoured her, running over her face, her shoulders, her breasts.

Her breath felt as if it were trapped in her chest. "You aren't going to ask me?"

The corner of his mouth lifted. "No."

Her gaze flew to his. He met her eyes, his body strung tight with lust. "Oliver," she said clearly. "Will you marry me?"

"Yes," he said. "Now kiss me."

Leaping at him, she took his mouth, kissing him with all the love and lust inside her. He kissed her back, wrapping his arms about her back and her thighs. Dimly, she realised he carried her to the chaise and he followed her down, pushing up her skirts as he reached for the fall of his breeches. Eagerly, she made room for him between her legs and they both groaned as he pressed against her, his hardness rubbing exactly right against her.

Suddenly, he pulled back. "Lydia," he said in a panic. "Lydia, I don't think I can wait."

She arched against him. "Neither can I."

"No, you don't understand. I have to...Lydia, this has to be good for you."

"It will be."

"Lydia, it will hurt you, and I don't think I can control myself—"

"Oliver." Grabbing handfuls of his glorious hair, she forced him to meet her gaze. Fear and panic and lust met her. "You will make this good for me."

"But what if—"

"Oliver," she said, and there was steel in her voice. "You will."

His gaze snapped to hers. "I will," he said thickly.

"Now." Curling his hair about his ears, she gave him a sweet smile. "Make me yours."

Eyes dark with returned lust, he ran his hands along her thighs and then between them. Pleasure melted through her, but she didn't break their gaze.

"You're wet," he said, his fingers playing over her. "You're so wet."

"Oliver," she gasped. "You. I want you. Not your hand."

"I know, but you have to be ready." His grin turned feral.

The fingers between her thighs rubbed, his thumb catching something and she wanted to scream. "Oliver, you—"

"Now," he said in satisfaction. "Now, you're ready."

She felt him against her entrance.

"Tell me if it hurts."

Skin tight, she nodded. He pushed inside and she inhaled sharply.

He froze. "Lydia?"

Nodding, she said, "Keep going."

He pushed another inch. It was all right, it was going to be all right— She inhaled again.

He stopped. He pushed and stopped, and let her get used to him before pushing again. He whispered against her ear, telling her she was beautiful and he loved her and he wanted her, *so much, Lydia, so damn much*, and then, finally, he was inside her

It felt...odd. It burned, and was slightly uncomfortable, and she felt...full. She was full of Oliver. A wild laugh built inside her.

"Lydia?" Features strained, he stared down at her.

She shifted underneath him and he closed his eyes, muttering a curse under his breath. It felt...better. The pleasure was returning with the knowledge Oliver was inside her. *Oliver was inside her.* "You may continue."

The arms braced on either side of her shook. "Christ, Lydia, don't make me laugh."

"I wasn't trying to," she said. "It feels better now, so I was telling you you may continue."

His features softened. Leaning down, he brushed her lips with his. "I love you."

His hips moved against her, pulling out only to push him back in. She wrapped her leg about his hip, enjoying the pleasure flicking over his face.

His gaze locked on hers. "What do you need?"

"What do you mean?"

"This has to be good for you, Lydia."

"It is good."

"No." He stopped moving, though it looked like it caused him pain. "You need more." Staying still inside her, he moved his hand between them to where they were joined. Gently, he brushed the sensitive bud above their joining.

Pleasure streaked through her. "Oh. Do that again."

He did. He did, he did, he did, and lightning streaked through her. He started moving again, thrusting in time with his touch, and it drove her mad, the pleasure too intense, and she moved with him, chasing something, chasing that pleasure he'd given her before. She moaned and bit and scratched and he groaned, panting that he was close, and she needed to come, *dear god, Lydia please come*, and she did. The pleasure blinded her, her body rigid, and he groaned in relief and bliss and he came too, he came inside her, and she loved him, she loved him so much.

The quiet in the room absorbed their harsh breathing. He lay atop her, still inside her, his face buried in her neck. She played with his hair, the long, glorious hair she loved.

After a time, he lifted his head to kiss her softly, his tongue lazily tangling with hers. Pulling back, he smiled at her, so sweetly her heart broke. She could never be without him again. "You're mine," she said fiercely.

He smiled, again so sweetly, and finally, he admitted, "I always was."

Epilogue

Eighteen years later…

LADY HOLLY FARLISLE LOOKED out over a carpet of white. Her bedchamber at Roxegate faced the London street, but winter and snow had dealt an eerie calm to the usually busy thoroughfare. She'd not seen a carriage for a good ten minutes or so, and no one had passed by on foot for even longer, bundled in warm cloaks and furs. Even the plethora of cousins on her mother's side who were similarly holed up in Torrence House had yet to brave the cold. Usually, they were running through the street, shrieking and throwing snowballs at each other, completely oblivious to the fact they were the children of a future Marquis and therefore Must Behave Properly, but then her family had always been odd.

"This is ridiculous," she said.

"What's ridiculous?" the Honourable Charlotte Farlisle asked. Her cousin lay on Holly's bed, throwing a cricket ball in the air which made a thwack sound each time she caught it.

"This." Gesturing at the window, she glared at the snow. "And Mama and Papa believing it a good idea to remain in London over the winter months."

"Oh," Charlotte replied, disinterest rampant in her tone.

"Oh? Is that all you have to say? Oh?"

Charlotte shrugged. "The Earl and the Countess of Roxwaithe are much in London and always hold Christmas here."

"They are your aunt and uncle, as well as my parents. You have no need to be so formal," Holly pointed out.

"My parents prefer the country. More ghosts for Mama to study," Charlotte said, and threw the cricket ball again.

"Come away from the window," her other cousin, the Honourable Davina Farlisle, ordered. "You are making me cold just standing there."

Defiantly, Holly turned to lean her back against the window, crossing her arms. Cold immediately invaded, but she refused to shiver.

"All our parents have decided to stay in London for winter," Davina continued. "And what's worse, they have decided we should all stay at Roxegate. All. Of. Us."

Davina had a point. Their family was large, with all their fathers having produced numerous children. She herself had three siblings, and her mother had the temerity to be with child once more. She was hoping for a brother this time, as she already had too many sisters to deal with.

She and her cousins had turned fifteen the previous spring, their birthdays within days of each other. While her mother didn't particularly care, she knew her aunt had started to pester Davina about preparing for their inevitable debuts. Charlotte's mother was too busy with her studies into the arcane and the spiritual to bother Charlotte about events that were years and years away, so Davina bore the brunt of dress fittings, lessons on deportment, and lectures on "Attracting Men" (always in quotation marks and capitalised), and then she reported back to Holly and Charlotte and cursed both of them when they laughed hysterically at her ire.

Movement in the street outside caught her eye. A carriage had arrived at the house opposite and a tall, lithe young man descended, hair of the purest gold peeking from the brim of his hat to curl over the collar of his great coat.

Her heart began to pound.

The young man walked up the stairs and the door swung open before he arrived. He said something to the butler, handing him his gloves and walking stick, then disappeared inside.

Pressing her arm into her stomach, she stared at the closed door. Her skin prickled and she felt slightly faint. Hugh Delancey had arrived home.

Most likely he'd arrived home after a night of debauchery. It was ten o'clock in the morning, and the only time she saw him before three in the afternoon was at the end of a debauch. She knew this because she'd been cataloguing his movements for years.

At twenty-six, Hugh was eleven years older than her and seemed to be enjoying his bachelorhood immensely. When gossip turned to him, she listened intently, desperate for even a scrap of information on him. She'd heard all about the wagers, the opera dancers, the wild parties. Her brother had quite explicitly told her she was to steer clear of men such as Hugh after she took her bow and entered her season. She had told him, in no uncertain terms, he had absolutely no jurisdiction in whom she chose to grace with her company and he was a dunderhead anyway.

The worst was the time she'd heard Hugh had been challenged to a duel. That had been horrible. She'd heard the rumour he was to meet Viscount Craigburn at dawn two days hence, and she wore her nails to the quick. Viscount Craigburn was a crack shot, and it wasn't until she'd seen Hugh arriving back at his town house, none the worse for wear, that she'd been able to breathe again.

She placed her hand on the window. Well. It seemed this crush wasn't going away. "I'm going to marry Hugh Delancey."

Charlotte missed catching the cricket ball, landing with a heavy thud on the floor.

Davina blinked. "Beg yours?"

"Hugh Delancey. I shall marry him. Two years after my debut, I should think. I should like to enjoy myself first."

"Hugh Delancey is too old," Charlotte scoffed.

"Just because Nicholas is only two years older than us doesn't mean everyone else is decrepit."

Charlotte's cheeks turned bright red. "You're decrepit," she mumbled.

She refused to dignify that with an answer.

"Putting age difference aside, there is the small fact he does not know you from Adam," Davina said.

Holly shrugged. "We've met."

"When?" she demanded.

"He lives across the street. Of course we've met." She didn't want to tell Davina every time she saw Hugh, an odd pulling sensation overcame her, as if he should always be by her side. Her heart sped, and her breath stopped, and she didn't know what to do with her hands. It was a bit frightening, the violence of the feeling, but she knew what it meant. Her mother had told her how she felt about her father. All that remained was to convince Hugh to admit he felt the same.

She'd seen how he'd looked at her, and then seen his self-disgust before he looked away. She knew he believed her too young and for the moment she was, but she wouldn't be young forever. There was a connection between them and, when she was old enough, they would be together.

Thus, when she turned eighteen, she made her bow. When she turned twenty, she cornered him and told him in no uncertain terms she meant to court him. He'd resisted, but she saw the longing in his eyes and so she'd ignored his half-hearted protests. After a week of determined courtship, he'd allowed her to see he felt the same love she had for him.

And so, when she was twenty-one, after a far too long engagement where she'd tempted him at every turn and he put up a valiant resistance only to fold like a cheap dress the night before their wedding, they married. And they lived happily ever after— except for when they fought, or when their children were annoying, or when she'd stupidly thought to have the servants clean out his pigsty of a study, or when he'd bought her a nosegay of petunias even though he should have known she reacted to them poorly, or when she was sick with their second child and he rubbed her swollen, aching feet, or when he caught a cold that became pneumonia and she was deathly afraid she would lose him, or when their son broke his arm falling from a tree, or when....

Acknowledgments

Thank you to the amazing A.L. Clark for your support, your editing skilz, and the re-introduction to roller coasters. I'm sorry I am a soulless monster who found them meh. Also, we totes need to write the eerie, fish-out-of-water, gangster, star-crossed lovers Gold Coast TV show. I'm certain Netflix are dying for our call.

To TP and the small humans you made, you peeps are my found family. I'm so privileged to have you in my life.

To my biological-ie-we-share-DNA-or-have-married-into family, you are the best. I'm also super privileged to have won that particular crap shoot.

This book would not exist with the outstanding authors involved in the Common Elements Romance Project. There are so many amazing stories in this project, I highly recommend you check them out.

And finally, as always, to you, the reader. Thank you for reading RESCUING LORD ROXWAITHE and if you have five minutes, it would be amazing if you would leave a review.

Until next time.

Read the third book in the Lost Lords series

STEALING LORD STEPHEN

The man she doesn't know she wants
A queen of the ton, Lady Seraphina Waller-Mitchell maintains her rule with a clever mind and a cutting tongue. A long-held rivalry leads her to attempt a seduction, but when the severely handsome lord proves difficult to beguile, Sera is forced to look beneath the surface...and finds a man who speaks to her soul.

The woman he doesn't know he needs
Lord Stephen Farlisle has no time for society. Followed by tragedy, he spends his privilege in helping those less fortunate, prowling Society's ballrooms to charm funds from deep pockets. When a striking beauty seeks a dalliance, Stephen dismisses her as a shallow flirt.

But when the two find themselves pretending courtship to win a wager, Stephen is fascinated by glimpses of the vulnerable woman beneath the mask, destroying preconceptions and prejudices...and threatening to steal his heavily guarded heart.

Read an Excerpt from
STEALING LORD STEPHEN
Lost Lords, Book Three

Chapter One

THE CARRIAGE JERKED OVER a bump in the road. Righting herself, Lady Seraphina Waller-Mitchell laced her fingers and stared straight ahead, her mind ticking over every step she would take that night.

She had no cause for nerves. This ball would be no different from any of the hundreds of balls she'd attended before. Indeed, she arranged each to her satisfaction, ensuring all would progress as it ought.

She would alight from her carriage and make her way to the entrance hall where she would be announced by the Pruitt's majordomo. Maria and Elizabeth would then attend her, having arrived at the ball prior to her as instructed. They would proceed to the southwest corner of the ballroom, which had the best aspect, and she would set up court, selectively choosing from those in attendance to provide amusement. She would bestow ten of the fourteen dances on six suitors of her choosing, forgoing four to instead observe and comment, and she would allow another suitor to bring her delicacies and punch. Elizabeth and Maria would relay the latest gossip, and from those in attendance she would determine on whom she would focus her efforts and her condescension. She had her strategy for a successful ball attendance and it would work, as it always did.

The carriage shuddered to a stop. The door opened and Jim appeared, the footman holding out his hand. "Good luck tonight, my lady."

Sera placed her hand in his, gathering her skirts in the other. "I don't need luck, Jim. I have a plan."

His lips twitched as he helped her descend. "Of course, my lady."

Setting her foot on the gravel, she sniffed. "Don't be impertinent, Jim. I should hate to have to terminate your employment, and it will do you no favours at this time of year. It would be next to impossible to find another position at this late stage, you know."

"Yes, my lady," he said mildly, as one who was often threatened with such and knew the threat to be completely toothless. Jim had been in her employ these eight years past, and she threatened to disengage him at least once a week.

To keep up the façade, she sniffed and then sailed into Pruitt House.

She had arrived almost two hours after the stated time on the invitation, as she had always intended, and thus the event was now a crush. Anyone who was anyone knew to arrive late was an absolute must, and she always added an extra half hour to ensure she was one of the last to arrive. People spilled from the ballroom into the entrance hall, down the corridors towards the cards and retiring rooms. Already the din was excruciating, the noise of hundreds in too small a place overwhelming.

Excitement stole the breath from her lungs. Finally, apprehension waned and she let the ball wash over her.

The majordomo stationed at the threshold to the ballroom nodded as she approached. "Lady Seraphina Waller-Mitchell," he announced.

His proclamation drew little notice from the crowd. Lifting her chin, she swept into the throng. It did not matter that she did not draw notice. She would, as always, make them notice.

Conversation and laughter melded into a cacophony, accompanied by the strains of the orchestra. The dancing had not yet commenced, ladies gossiping behind their fans while gentlemen pretended they did not listen in earnest. Lady Pruitt had chosen a Greek theme for her ball, with marble columns and drapery. Grottos had been created from columns and greenery, the most elaborate housing the orchestra. The grotto with the next best vantage stood on the other side of the ballroom and was already occupied. Four young girls, debutantes all, whispered and giggled where Sera had planned to be.

Annoyance drew her brows. Elizabeth and Maria had been under strict instructions to reserve the grotto with the best vantage. Stern words would be exchanged once she rectified the situation.

Arriving at the grotto that should be hers, Sera arranged a pretty smile on her features. "Good evening."

The girls stopped talking. "Lady Seraphina," one exclaimed.

Regally, she inclined her head. "My dears, I find myself confused as to why you have taken occupation of this area of the ballroom."

They glanced amongst themselves. One of them said hesitantly, "Lady Seraphina, we thought—"

"This grotto is not to your best vantage," she interrupted. "You would do well to remove to the eastern corner of the room, close to the orchestra. The gentlemen always gravitate that way."

They glanced at each other excitedly. "Oh, thank you, Lady Seraphina, thank you."

"Of course, my dears. Only too happy to help."

Breathlessly talking amongst themselves of which gentleman would take note of them, who would have the first dance, and those things that thrilled debutantes at their first ball, the girls departed.

Slapping her fan in her hand, Sera dropped her smile. Now *she* had the best vantage.

Taking their position framed by the grotto, she flicked her wrist and fanned herself absently as she surveyed the crowd. There was a shocking proliferation of bright colour: reds and blues, oranges and pinks. Lace and ruffles choked gowns, and after years of muslin and cotton, some had ventured into expensive silks. Her own gown lacked embellishment, but that would only make her stand out from the crowd. Should she also change her colour palette? Currently she wore a rather muted shade of blue, designed to bring out the chestnut highlights in her dark brown hair and the blue flecks in her grey eyes, but perhaps she should go bolder. Maybe this year her signature colour *would* be blue, but with shades ranging from robin's egg and periwinkle to royal and navy.

From across the ballroom, a girl stared openly at her.

Sera frowned. Was the girl simple? There were ways to observe without being obvious about it. Tilting her head, she observed the girl from the corner of her eye. Clearly foreign with brown skin and dark hair, she was dressed in the very height of London fashion, the deep yellow of her gown complementing her skin and setting off her dark eyes. That appeared to be the sum total of her intrigue. She stood with no one of note, and she had attracted little notice from anyone who was anyone.

Dismissing her, Sera continued her perusal.

"Lady Seraphina, a delight as always."

How very tiresome. "Your grace," she said flatly.

The Duke of Sutton offered her what no doubt would be termed a charming smirk, one that said he knew of his attractiveness—with his wealth and his title and his handsomeness—and he also knew one should be flattered he deigned to acknowledge you. "Come, my dear, surely we have a greater acquaintance than that? Last year, you called me Sutton."

"That was last year," she said dismissively.

"Last year, you also permitted…familiarities."

Was he going to be tiresome about everything? "As I said, that was last year."

"What has changed between then and now?" he asked silkily.

"For one, the year."

The slightest of frowns touched his forehead. "Why are you being so difficult?"

Annoyance began to swirl within her. He knew the rules of the game. They had enjoyed a flirtation, one that benefited them both and had always had an expiry. The Duke of Sutton was notorious for his flirtations and the trail of broken hearts he left behind; he was ruthless, unfeeling, and had made many a lady weep. Why was he attempting to prolong what had already died? "I am not difficult, your grace. I am bored. There is a difference."

"Bored? Bored? With *me*?"

She exhaled. "I am no longer interested. You may leave."

"You? Are dismissing *me*?"

With a snap of her wrist, she extended her fan and proceeded to ignore him.

"You will regret this," he threatened.

She flicked him a glance. "Will I?"

He smiled tightly and then, finally, he let her be, disappearing into the crowd.

Ugh, now her stomach was twisted in knots. Why did the duke have to approach her? Her plan for the ball had not included his histrionics, and she hadn't required his petty threats. Fanning herself rhythmically, she breathed in, and then out. In, out. Slowly, the churn in her stomach subsided.

Her gaze locked on two familiar faces amongst the crowd. Lady Elizabeth Harcourt and Miss Maria Spencer froze, their faces draining of colour as they noticed her glare. Quickly, they hurried to her side.

"Lady Seraphina," Elizabeth exclaimed. "You are early!"

"I? *I* am early?"

Elizabeth blanched. "We are late?" she offered.

"I told you both *precisely* when I would be here. Imagine my surprise upon arrival when I discovered not only were you absent, but the position I had chosen specifically for this first ball was occupied by first years."

They glanced at each other. "We apologise," Maria said. "However, you will not mind when we tell you what Margaret Williamson told us—"

"It does not matter what Margaret Williamson told you. I specifically instructed you reserve this grotto and you did not do so."

"But Margaret Williamson told us—"

Sera held up her hand. Maria fell silent. "I do not care what you discovered."

Maria opened her mouth. "But—"

Narrowing her eyes, Sera shot her a look.

"The Marchioness Demartine, Lady Alexandra Torrence, Lady Lydia Torrence," the majordomo intoned.

Sera whipped around. Lips pressed together, she watched as Lady Demartine entered the ballroom flanked by her daughters.

"That's what we were trying to tell you. Lydia Torrence is back." Elizabeth said weakly.

Ignoring Elizabeth, Sera kept her gaze trained on the new arrivals. Lady Demartine was still a beauty, her dark brows a curious contrast with her pale hair. Neither of her daughters had inherited her colouring, with Lady Alexandra's hair a more golden shade of blonde and Sera knew her eyes to be of a muddy sort. Lydia's hair was red, her eyes bright blue-green hazel. Some seemed to think Lydia was beautiful.

Sera gritted her teeth. Fine, Lydia *was* beautiful. Red-gold hair tumbled around her head, her features perfect, with a curvaceous figure just a shade on the right side of ladylike. The gentlemen would flock to her side, but if her affections remained as they had always been, they were doomed to disappointment.

Lady Alexandra was the same age as Sera but had made her debut the year after her. Sera smiled thinly. And what a disaster it had been. Lady Alexandra was…odd. She was fascinated by spirits and cared not who knew it. She was exuberant in everything she did—too bright, too eager, too *much*. It would bear her well if she was just…less.

Sera's gaze slid again to Lydia. Lady Lydia Torrence, recently returned from an extended tour of the Continent. She seemed to have gained polish and poise, and an easy confidence that would draw others to her. That, coupled with her ridiculous beauty, would make her the hit of the Ton. No longer wide-eyed, her thoughts were disguised behind a faintly amused smile. Her smile brightened, however, when her gaze lit upon Lady Violet Crafers. With a quick word to her mother, she crossed the ballroom to join Lady Violet, her smile genuine as she reached her friend's side.

"There is a rumour the Earl of Roxwaithe will be in attendance as well."

"Hmm?" She glanced at Elizabeth.

"Alice Stamford said she heard it from Georgina Parkerson, who heard it from Caroline Bennett, and you know Caroline Bennett knows everything," Elizabeth continued.

"He *never* attends balls," Maria breathed.

"He sometimes attends," Sera said absently. Her mind raced. That would not be why, though. It wasn't a coincidence the earl chose to attend just as Lydia Torrence made her return.

Once, forever ago, she'd been friendly with Lydia Torrence and the girl had taken her in confidence, telling her of her life-long crush on the earl. The earl, though, was fourteen years Lydia's elder and clearly would not be interested in a girl barely seventeen who he no doubt regarded as a much younger sister. Sera, helpfully, had informed Lydia of this and had attempted to turn her from such a fruitless affection. She had, quite helpfully, told others of Lydia's crush, to show the girl how ridiculous it was. Lydia, though, had overreacted to her kind action, screaming and crying and declaring Sera a terrible fiend.

Their friendship had soured after that.

"The earl *is* in attendance," Maria breathed.

"Where?" Sera searched the ballroom.

"There." Maria pointed.

Sure enough, the Earl of Roxwaithe had entered the ballroom. Sera frowned over his appearance. He was so...hairy. Long golden-brown hair was tied back in a knot at the nape of his neck, while his jaw was covered by a beard. He was so...unusual. Few gentlemen of her acquaintance had hair of his length, and none sported a beard

His gaze immediately sought out Lydia Torrence. She had not yet seen him, and he seemed to drink her in. Possibly it was the first time he had seen her since her return, but in any event he displayed his emotion as clearly as if he had shouted.

Some years after the incident with Lydia, it had become apparent Sera had been mistaken in her assessment of the earl. He clearly returned Lydia's affections, and that gave Sera all the ammunition she needed to taunt Lydia—who just as clearly had no clue—at every turn.

She smiled thinly. One did not spurn Lady Seraphina Waller-Mitchell and not live to regret it.

Unaware of Sera's thoughts, Elizabeth asked, "Will you choose a gentleman this year?"

"Don't I always?" Every year it amused her to choose a gentleman to flirt with and beguile. Last year it had been the Duke of Sutton. This year... Her gaze drifted to Lydia Torrence. "Perhaps I will entertain myself with an earl this season."

"An earl?" Maria asked in confusion.

"The Earl of Roxwaithe, Maria. Honestly." Sometimes she questioned why she associated with them.

Elizabeth frowned. "But he is never in society, Sera. There is no point."

"He will attend enough this season," she said dismissively.

"How do you know?"

Lydia Torrence was here and it followed the Earl of Roxwaithe would be where she is. "It is a feeling. Do not distract me." She levelled her gaze on the earl.

Still he watched Lydia Torrence. They both couldn't be more obvious if they tried. It would be pointless to attempt to attract his attention. While she enjoyed a challenge, she did not enjoy failure and that way lay nothing but frustration. However, if she remembered correctly, the earl had a brother. "What is the name of the younger brother to the Earl of Roxwaithe?"

Maria blinked. "The one who is dead?" she asked hesitantly.

"No." She remembered his name, of course. Everyone remembered that tragedy. Lord Maxim Farlisle, the youngest of the brothers, lost at sea these eight years past. What he had been doing on a ship to the Americas to begin with had caused furious speculation amongst the Ton at the time, though none could determine exactly why he had sought that passage. "The one who is alive."

Elizabeth and Maria exchanged glances and then gave her blank looks.

Impatience made her tone harsh. "Well?"

"I do not know, Seraphina," Elizabeth said hastily.

"He plays football on a heath outside the city," Maria offered.

Sera's brows shot up. "The brother of an earl? Playing football? In *public*? How do you know this?"

Maria blanched. "I—I don't know. I just do."

"But you do not know his name?"

"Stephen!" Triumph lit Maria's expression. "It is Stephen!"

Lord Stephen Farlisle. "Is he in attendance this evening?"

Maria opened her mouth but uttered no sound. Elizabeth bit her lip.

Honestly, did she have to do everything herself? "Lady Asterd knows everyone and everything. Go find her."

They scurried to do her bidding. Sera returned her contemplation to the earl pretending he did not watch Lady Lydia while she pretended she took no notice of him at all.

In short order, Maria returned, breathless. "Lady Asterd said he attends this evening. He is in the ballroom."

Sera immediately turned her gaze to the throng. "Where?"

Maria searched. "There," she said, pointing.

On the opposite side of the ballroom, a lone gentleman stood, seemingly disinclined to change that state. He was unimpressive, for all he was tall, and though his shoulders were broad he was far too slender for her liking. His clothing was sombre and did not mould to his form, and his unsmiling face was not handsome: his brow too high, his nose too bold, his jaw too strong. His mouth, however, was full and sensual, his lips plush and sulky and the only softness in that harsh face. Blond hair did not riot in a tumble of curls as other gentlemen's did, the short, straight strands pomaded close to his skull. She could not determine his eye colour from this distance, but she would wager a guinea it was some shade of brown. What shade she would determine that upon engineering their acquaintance.

She frowned. From the depths of her memory, she recalled him from her first—or was it her second?—season. He had been merry and dashing and wicked, and he and his friends had delighted in thumbing their noses at the strictures of society. His clothing had been the pip of fashion, his hair the careless tumble of curls one could only achieve with hours of styling. Then he had disappeared for some time, and talk of scandal had emerged, something about carriages and duels and maybe even a death? The gossip had died down, as it always did, and she had promptly forgotten about him.

Until now. Now, he served a purpose. Now, he would facilitate her irritating Lydia Torrence.

Dismissing those barely recalled memories, she focused instead on the present. No doubt she would discover more as their acquaintance progressed and, if it was relevant, she would address it then.

"Where did you find Lady Asterd?" she asked.

"With the other matrons in the retiring room. Why?"

"I require an introduction and, as I said, Lady Asterd knows everyone."

Maria frowned. "But Sera, Lady Asterd does not like you."

"I know." Affecting a dazzling smile, she asked, "I am put together?"

Still frowning, Maria replied, "Of course."

"Make sure we retain the grotto," Sera instructed and then she swept away to find Lady Asterd.

She had a man to beguile.

Chapter Two

LORD STEPHEN FARLISLE WAS doing his level best to avoid the Earl of Roxwaithe. It wasn't too hard a feat. His brother didn't seem inclined to associate with him either.

Exhaling, he cast his gaze around the ballroom. Usually, he avoided balls and assemblies like the plague, but the coffers of the foundation were never deep enough and a ball might mean members of the Ton were more inclined to reach into their pockets. If he could get them to throw some guineas his way, he could endure an hour or two.

Raising his hand, he stifled a yawn. He'd been up since half five that morning and, as the clocks now rapidly approached midnight, he was battling to stay awake. Knowing he was to attend the ball this evening, he should have forced himself to remain in bed, but he found it hard to sleep in, his body now well used to rising with the sun. Every morning, at a little past sunrise, he made his way out to the heath. Few milled about at that hour, and thus there were none to see as he performed the morning exercises that had become his routine. He didn't mind the stretching and running, but the shock of the water as he swam in the heath's freezing lake was uniformly bracing. The lifting of weights, though, he truly despised. These past four days, he'd neglected the exercise and he was paying for it now. If it weren't for the fact his body would seize even more, and it would be that much harder to get himself back to half as good, he would be thankful to never again perform such a vile exercise.

Subtly, he rotated his shoulders. They were aching a little, old injuries making themselves known. He'd dislocated his shoulder six months ago on the pitch, and though it had mostly healed, it troubled him at odd moments. However, it was merely one ache amongst many, and newer than the rest. He'd had these last seven years or more to get used to a body that didn't always work as it should, and lingering aches and pains that reminded him of past recklessness and stupidity.

Across from him, Lord Gray entered the ballroom. Finally, one of the reasons Stephen had attended had arrived. Lord Gray had more wealth than he knew what to do with and the rumour was he would gift to anyone with a half-decent story.

Setting his step toward Lord Gray, he recited yet again his appeal in his head. He'd practiced all of yesterday and today, with variations depending on whom he would be pitching it to. "Lord Gray," he greeted.

His lordship turned. "Yes?"

"Lord Stephen Farlisle, my lord."

His brow creased. "Who?"

Christ. "Roxwaithe's brother," he reluctantly clarified.

Recognition lit Lord Gray's expression. Of course it bloody did. Everyone knew his bloody brother. "Ah, Roxwaithe. Good man. And you're his brother?"

Stephen held on to his pleasant expression. "Yes."

"Good. Good. Damned crush, this. Can't put two thoughts together."

Pushing aside his ire, Stephen continued, "I wonder if I might bend your ear on an investment opportunity."

"What? Loud as the dickens in here."

Stephen raised his voice. "An investment opportunity, but also a charitable one."

"What? Charity? Don't know much about that. Have to ask Lady Gray on that one. She's the one who likes doffing out coin on unfortunates."

"This is both, Gray."

"An investment, you say?" Gray looked him over. "Discussed this investment with your brother?"

Stephen gritted his teeth. "Of course." In that he'd mentioned his intention to form a foundation to his brother once in passing and Oliver had grunted in return.

"Always gets in on the ground floor, Roxwaithe. Doubled his fortune, rumour has it."

"My brother is astute." And miserly, and judgemental, and an all around arse.

"Yes, well, better at managing dosh, isn't he? *Doubled* his fortune." He nodded sagely.

Stephen's hands curled to fists. Lord Gray didn't mean that as a dig. The man clearly didn't know anything about Stephen's own fortune, or to be precise, his lack of one. "Shall I attend you tomorrow, Gray?"

"If you want. Will make sure her ladyship is also present. She's the one who likes charities, what." Lord Gray's gaze drifted past him.

Stephen knew when to retreat. "Thank you, Gray," he said and, with a stiff bow, he left.

As he circled the ballroom, he consulted his pocket watch. Twenty more minutes and it would not be untoward of him to leave. With one opportunity gained, the ball wasn't a complete waste.

Absently, he rotated his wrist, the action not entirely fluid. Once, he'd lived for amusement, the wilder the better. Who would have thought at the age of almost thirty-one he would be desirous most of his bed? And what's more, to be alone in it.

From across the ballroom, a woman stared.

He stared back. A small smile played about her rosebud mouth as she noticed his regard. Dark hair piled atop her head, a few tendrils teasing a long, creamy neck that flowed into straight shoulders and an impressive bosom.

Stephen kept his expression impassive. Her name sat on the tip of his tongue and he was certain he would have been introduced to her at one point or another. However, his first season had been spent in pursuit of reckless decadence, and the second he'd hied to the Continent with Harbor. His third and fourth... He'd been unable to do much of anything in what would have been his third and fourth.

Flicking her fan open, her gaze met his over the top of it, one delicate brow arching.

His own brows drew into a frown. Was she flirting with him?

"Lord Stephen," a soft voice beside him said.

He stiffened. Ah, bollocks. "Good evening, my lady."

Lady Demartine's expression was faintly chiding. "It has been an age since I have seen you, Lord Stephen," she gently rebuked.

"I have been...busy," he said lamely.

"Too busy to even enjoy a cup of tea?"

He opened his mouth to say again he'd been busy but that chiding expression halted him. Lady Demartine was as a mother to him, and as his had died when he was a child, she was the only mother he knew. He *hated* disappointing her.

"I have missed you, Stephen," she said. "Demartine and I both."

"Yes, my lady."

She looped her arm through his. "Take a turn with me and tell me what you have been up to."

"Nothing," he said as they began their tour.

"Ah, you men," she said, a smile in her voice. "All of you are the same. You say you never do anything and then, five minutes later, one cannot stop your talk of everything and anything. How is your football team?"

"They—we—go well."

"And the children you teach?

"Coach, Lady Demartine. It is called coaching."

"Ah. The children you coach, how are they?"

"Also well."

Her mouth kicked up. "Perhaps I was wrong, Stephen. Perhaps you do not speak of everything and anything."

He ducked his head again, this time to conceal a smile. "How are you, my lady?"

"Ah, changing the subject. Well played, Stephen," she teased.

Though his cheeks heated, his grin widened. Lady Demartine always saw straight through him.

"When was the last time you saw your brother?"

His smile died abruptly. "I don't know."

She shook her head. "You two. You would think with everything that has occurred you would be closer."

"He started it," he said sullenly, and then cursed himself for the childish remark.

Lady Demartine's knowing gaze weighted heavy upon him. "I daresay you are both old enough to handle your relationship yourselves, even if you do not act like it." She sighed. "At least we see you at a ball. Perhaps treat your brother kindly, though. There is much to which he has had to adjust."

His hands clenched into fists. "And he? Should he treat me kindly?"

Surprised lit her expression. "He does, Stephen."

He shrugged.

Shaking her head, she said again, "You two."

Clenching his jaw, he took a breath. Lady Demartine meant well, he knew. "I beg your pardon, madam, but I find myself in need of refreshment."

She gazed at him levelly. "Do you?" she finally said.

His neck heated again. How did she always know when he was prevaricating?

She shook her head. "No matter. Go, Stephen. I shan't keep you when you don't want to converse."

Bowing sharply, he departed, pretending he couldn't feel her gaze between his shoulder blades as he left. The refreshment room held nothing stronger than an orgeat lemonade, and he grimaced as he drank. He'd never liked the flavour, and it was especially bad when watered down in this manner. Handing his cup to a footman, he blanched as he was accosted by a whirl of ruffles and lace.

"Lord Stephen!" Lady Asterd cried.

He winced. "Lady Asterd."

A matronly woman loosely acquainted with Lady Demartine, Lady Asterd had in seasons past introduced him to numerous eligible debutantes in an attempt to match-make. She had been decidedly unsuccessful.

"Thank goodness I found you before that vile girl did," she exclaimed.

His brows shot up. Lady Asterd was not known for her subtlety, but even that was a bit much.

"I would never forgive myself if I allowed you to fall in her clutches. It would cause my dear friend such distress, and Lady Demartine has had too many tragedies in her life. Why, there was poor, lost Maxim, of course." Producing a handkerchief from her gown, she held it to her eye.

"Of course." Because the death of his younger brother eleven years ago did not affect him, Stephen, in any way at all.

"And your dear mother. Such friends we were, though I was a little older than them. Bosom companions, always together at each ball. They even married within months of each other and then, for your poor mother to pass bringing your poor brother into the world, and then he departing not a dozen years later—"

"Maxim was fifteen," he interrupted.

Her ladyship blinked. "Pardon?"

Lady Asterd had no notion what she said could be upsetting to him, and he couldn't be bothered explaining it to her. "Nothing, Lady Asterd. You were saying something about a girl?"

"Yes! Lady Seraphina Waller-Mitchell! Do not fall for her wicked wiles, Lord Stephen."

Never, in all his life, had he fallen prey to a woman's wiles. When he was younger, he knew the game and he played it well. Now...it all seems so false, and he had no time for falsity. Except when it came to his brother. He would prevaricate and obfuscate until the cows came home for Oliver. "I shall be sure not to do so, my lady."

"Good. Good. She is a wicked sort, that one."

A spark of interest flared; Lady Asterd's vehemence almost made him want to seek the woman out to see what was so very wicked about her. Almost. "Thank you, I shall take your words under advisement."

She nodded importantly. "Good. Good. I could not bear it if something happened and I did not warn you."

"Of course," he said ironically.

Her gaze flitted past him. "Oh, I must—Lady Walpole! My apologies, Lord Stephen, but— Lady Walpole!"

Rolling his shoulders, he watched as she rushed away to accost Lady Walpole. Thank Christ that was over. Lady Asterd was tolerable in small doses—very small doses.

From across the ballroom, the woman smiled at him archly. Lady Seraphina Waller-Mitchell. Wickedness personified, apparently.

Behind her, staring at Lydia Torrence like the obvious clodpole he was, stood Oliver. Christ, he had no desire to be forced to converse with his brother. Turning on his heel, Stephen departed the ballroom.

The balcony was fairly deserted for such a crowded ball. A few gentlemen smoked, and some ladies gathered to take in the night air. Stephen found a deserted corner and leant against the balustrade, inhaling evening blossoms, perfume, and cheroot smoke. A hint of rain threaded the air, speaking of summer storms.

He rubbed a hand across his face. He didn't know if he had it in him to take another pass around the ballroom. He was not used to society and, it was plain, society was not used to him.

Someone stumbled into him, a whirl of pale blue. Automatically he caught her, dark hair bobbing at his chin as she gripped his forearms.

"Thank you, my lord," she said breathily. Still gripping him, she looked up.

He drew in a breath. It was the woman from the ballroom. The wicked one.

Tilted grey eyes framed with thick dark lashes stared up at him from a heart-shaped face. A pale blue gown clothed her, the square neckline framing truly magnificent breasts...though he questioned how much was her and how much clever undergarments. Interestingly, though, she was no more than a head shorter than him, and he was accounted a tall man

Expression coy, she gazed at him through her lashes. "However can I thank you, sir? You have saved me from a dire fate."

"A slight stumble is a dire fate?"

Her brow creased slightly before clearing, a dazzling smile taking its place. "What could be worse than a lady tearing her hem?"

"What indeed," he murmured. Clearly, she had performed this apparent artlessness a hundred times and, just as clearly, it usually worked. It was...affecting, he granted her. Play the damsel in distress and position him as the triumphant hero. If he'd had a different frame of mind, it might have even worked. As it was, he saw straight through her ploy. Why she'd chosen him out of all the gentlemen he couldn't say.

Her smile slipped somewhat as he declined to comment further. "But as I said, I must thank you."

"There is no need."

"Surely there is some way I can show my gratitude?" Her smile was an alluring mix of innocence and archness. Lady Asterd had been right. This woman and wickedness were well-acquainted.

His own wickedness prompted him. "Do you often find this works?" he asked conversationally.

Her smile froze. "I beg your pardon?"

"The helpless damsel seeking the assistance of a big, brave, strong gentleman. What is next? Will you insinuate the promise of a kiss only to deny it? We are, after all, in full view of the ballroom."

She drew in a sharp breath, her grey eyes wide.

"You play this game well, I admit," he continued. "I would even warrant most would not even know they were playing counterpart. It is admirable."

Scowling, she set herself from him and pulled herself straight. She forgot to position herself to best advantage, her cheeks pinkening as she struggled to contain her ire. He watched, fascinated. This woman was vastly more interesting.

"*You*," she spat, "are not acting as you ought."

"Oh? And how ought I act?"

"With respect. With dignity. With *gentlemanly* concern."

Enjoying himself immensely, he twisted the knife. "I was unaware this was my role."

"You should be flattered by my attention. Flattered! Do you know who I am? What my condescension means?"

"Clearly, I do not."

"I am sought after. I am the one everyone wishes to know. My favour has the ability to make or break a season."

He shrugged.

She looked as if she would explode. "You are no gentleman."

"I never claimed otherwise."

"You are so vexing!"

"I did not think I could inspire such passion on so short an acquaintance."

"And yet, you have," she replied snidely.

"Perhaps, then, you should focus your attention on another more worthy."

Abruptly, her passion faded and her eyes narrowed. "Should I?"

Unease skittered through him. Somehow, he had lost control...but then, what did he care? He had left this game long ago and he had no desire to return. She was interesting, he granted, and perhaps if he was as he had been, he would have enjoyed sparring with her. But he wasn't as he had been. Too much had happened for him to ever be that foolish and selfish again. "I find I have had enough of the air. I bid you good evening." Bowing sharply, he made for the French doors.

"You are leaving?" she said, disbelief threading her tone.

"As I said."

"You can't just *leave*. You are not—"

He didn't hear the end of her sentence, the din of chatter and laugher as he entered the ball drowning out her words. He was at this ball for one reason: to raise funds. She had made him forget, and that he could not allow.

Setting his shoulders, he made for the richest pockets he could pick.

Read the first book in the Lost Lords series

FINDING LORD FARLISLE

The boy she never forgot
Lady Alexandra Torrence knows she's odd. Fascinated by spirits, she sets out to investigate rumours of a ghost at Waithe Hall, the haunt of her childhood. Its shuttered corridors stir her own ghosts: memories of the friend she'd lost. Maxim had been her childhood playmate, her kindred spirit, the boy she was beginning to love ...but then he'd abandoned her, only to be lost at sea. She never expected to stumble upon a handsome and rough-hewn man who had made the Hall his home, a man she is shocked to discover is Maxim: alive, older...and with no memory of her.

The girl he finally remembers
Eleven years ago, a shipwreck robbed Lord Maxim Farlisle of his memory. Finally remembering himself, he journeys to his childhood home to find Waithe Hall shut and deserted. Unwilling to face what remains of his family, Maxim makes his home in the abandoned hall only to have a determined beauty invade his uneasy peace. This woman insists he remember her and slowly, he does. Once, he and Alexandra had been inseparable, beloved friends who were growing into something more...but the reasons he left still exist, and how can he offer her a broken man?

As the two rediscover their connection, the promise of young love burns into an overwhelming passion. But the time apart has scarred them both—will they discover a love that binds them together, or will the past tear them apart forever?

TEACH ME

Ever curious, Elizabeth, Viscountess Rocksley, has turned her curiosity to erotic pleasure. Three years a widow, she boldly employs the madam of a brothel for guidance but never had she expected her education to be conducted by a coldly handsome peer of the realm.

To the Earl of Malvern, the erotic tutelage of a skittish widow is little more than sport, however the woman he teaches is far from the mouse he expects. With her sly humor and insistent joy, Elizabeth obliterates all his expectations and he, unwillingly fascinated, can't prevent his fall.

Each more intrigued than they are willing to admit, Elizabeth and Malvern embark upon a tutelage that will challenge them, change them, come to mean everything to them...until a heartbreaking betrayal threatens to tear them apart forever.

SILK & SCANDAL
The Silk Series, Book 1

Eight years ago...
Thomas Cartwright and Lady Nicola Fitzgibbons were friends. Over the wall separating their homes, Thomas and Nicola talked of all things – his studies to become a barrister, her frustrations with a lady's limitations.

All things end.
When her diplomat father gains a post in Hong Kong, Nicola must follow. Bored and alone, she falls into scandal. Mired in his studies of the law and aware of the need for circumspection, Thomas feels forced to sever their ties.

But now Lady Nicola is back…and she won't let him ignore her.

About Cassandra Dean

Cassandra Dean is an award-winning author of historical and fantasy romance. She grew up daydreaming, inventing fantastical worlds and marvelous adventures. Once she learned to read (First phrase – To the Beach. True story), she was never without a book, reading of other people's fantastical worlds and marvelous adventures.

Cassandra is proud to call South Australia her home, where she regularly cheers on her AFL football team and creates her next tale.

Connect with Cassandra

cassandradean.com

facebook.com/AuthorCassandraDean

twitter.com/authorCassDean

instagram.com/authorcassdean

bookbub.com/authors/cassandra-dean

To learn about exclusive content, upcoming releases and giveaways,
join Cassandra's mailing list:

cassandradean.com/extras/subscribe

Made in United States
Orlando, FL
26 May 2022